GERARD KLEIN...

. . . probably the best science fiction writer in France today, loves to write novels of the intricacies of time and the vastness of the universe. He is also fascinated by the game of chess, of which he is a master.

The French title of this newly translated novel could be said to be *The Killers of Time*. But is misleading. This edge-of-the-seat sf-thriller is far too fast moving for that sort of suggestion.

Here we have a starliner traveling from the Lesser Magellanic Cloud metagalaxy to our Milky Way system about a million or more years from now. It falls into the crossfire of two unseen fleets originating millions of years in the starliner's own future —near the end of the universe. The starliner, unseen by either combatant, is thrown backwards into an earlier epoch—millions of years before Earth and its sun existed. How does it manage to return to its own period? And what did it do to the contest of which it was an unnoticed victim?

We finally found a title that would fit its special character. We call it . . .

THE MOTE IN TIME'S EYE.

THE MOTE IN TIME'S EYE

Gerard Klein

Translated by
C. J. RICHARDS

DAW BOOKS, INC.

DONALD A. WOLLHEIM, PUBLISHER

1301 Avenue of the Americas
New York, N. Y.   10019

Cover art by Josh Kirby.

"Quand Dieu a créé le temps, il en a créé beaucoup . . ."

Translated by C. J. Richards.

FIRST PRINTING, JANUARY 1975

1 2 3 4 5 6 7 8 9

PRINTED IN U.S.A.

CHAPTER I

The spaceship was approaching the end of a profit-able twelve-year voyage of exploration. It was halfway between the two Magellanic Clouds.

This had been the most daring expedition the human civilization of the Lesser Magellanic Cloud had ever sent forth. Its supreme magistrates had had great vision, believing that their interests required it.

Their forebears had come from the Prime-Galaxy, five or six thousand years earlier. They had quickly conquered new worlds and increased their population. In the year 27,937 (universal base) when this story begins, the human civilization of the Lesser Magellanics consisted of about six thousand planets with an average population of roughly two hundred and fifty thousand. On some worlds, there were almost one hundred mil-lion people; on others, there was just a handful of families.

Men could still be comfortable in the Lesser Magel-lanic Cloud system. They could continue to multiply at the same rate for about twenty thousand years before reaching the limit of the stellar nebula. But this did not prevent them from going to see what was happening beyond their own system. Their interest in unknown worlds tended to increase with distance.

The ship was spherical. It could travel one million light-years in one year. When it left Neo-Sirius, it had a crew of six thousand. Twelve years later, taking into account births and deaths, it carried 7,591. There was room for over ten thousand on board. The power of the ship's generators and weaponry was considerable; nevertheless, considering the distance and the obstacles, the *Vasco* was nothing but an eggshell.

The *Vasco* was returning home after twelve years. The last eighteen months of navigation had proceeded without mishap, in known space. There was no mass of stellar importance to impede the ship's progress within a hundred light-years. The direction detectors had remained silent; had the robots been capable of boredom they would have sounded an electronic complaint. There had been enormous risks earlier, but the people of the Magellanics were adventurous. And the hold of the *Vasco*, packed with booty, was proof enough of the advantages of taking risks in space.

There was nothing on board the *Vasco* to indicate that it had been crossing the biggest battlefield in history for thousands of light-years.

The ships which were in conflict—we'll call them ships for lack of a better word, but they bore practically no similarity to the sort of craft the *Vasco* was—lurked in areas of space where the *Vasco's* detectors could not reach. Although the battle had been raging for over seven thousand years, its front was still spreading. In fact, the battlefield had shifted constantly throughout time. The war had started, as far as the *Vasco* was concerned, in a future so remote that its passengers could have no concept of it. The adversaries were two galactic cumulae and two powerful races.

In theory, allowance had been made for the possible accidental incursion of ships foreign to both sides into the battlefield; the non-belligerents were not even supposed to suspect that they were going through a battlefield. But somewhere, a mistake had been made.

A series of unlucky circumstances had propelled the *Vasco* into the very center of the battle. First it had gone through a zone in which a "cruiser" had exploded, thereby shattering the innermost structures of space.

Then it had slipped out of Second Space, while going through it, into a multidirectional area. There it was immediately picked up by an unmanned receiving station which proceeded to surround it, as a measure of precaution, with a minefield. Had the *Vasco's* detectors been equipped to pick up these objects and had Captain Shangrin had any idea of the risks his ship was running, he would immediately have stopped the engines; but he had no reason to suspect that anything was amiss.

Nor did the station's warnings alert him: the field which ought to have inhibited ordinary enemy generators was ineffectual against the primitive motors of the *Vasco*. Finally, the ship passed at less than one light-year from a mine and set it off. Without a sound, without a tremor, the *Vasco* was instantly projected into the past.

The unmanned station signaled immediately to the proper authority that a foreign ship of unknown origin had been withdrawn from circulation. The situation was considered so serious that any inquiry was postponed, there being more urgent problems to be dealt with.

Nevertheless, an abridged account of the incident was sent to headquarters. At the same moment, sixteen million other messages, from different sources, were pouring into the central computer bank which, because it was beginning to show signs of overwork, did not pick out the *Vasco* incident. This would not have been of any consequence had it not been for the peculiar makeup of the Magellanites.

Captain Varun Shangrin was the commandant of the *Vasco*. The supreme magistrates of the sixteen sponsoring planets of the Magellanic Cloud had hesitated a long time before hiring him to lead the expedition they were financing.

True, he came from a family which had explored many virgin planets. He had knocked about in countless sectors of space. He had always brought back his ships with their crews. This last was the deciding factor, for the magistrates quaked at the mere possibility of giving back to space the tremendous fortunes that had been wrenched from it.

But Shangrin was reputed to be an adventurer,

quick-tempered to the point of violence. His voice could make the stars tremble. He was said to be a galley master rather than a captain, an eager warlord, a man who enjoyed life to the full. The supreme magistrates of the Lesser Magellanic Cloud shivered in their comfortable houses as they remembered Varun Shangrin's exploits and his laughter. Privately they referred to him as a pirate, a space brigand, a pillager, and thought him the repository of all vices. But they knew they could launch him into the unknown, sure that he would come back laden with riches, fired up with novel schemes, his eyes reflecting the glories of new and fabulous worlds.

He made them nervous because he was a truly great leader and a better businessman than they were. He would walk into their elegantly appointed offices, helmeted, booted, trailing the chill of outer space and the smell of machinery, and then coerce them into risking their money in exchange for an uncertain hope. He would leave them panting for months and years, but he would come back unchanged, tanned by giant suns. He made them nervous because what he risked was his life; they risked only their fortunes. And they were afraid of him because he often made outlandish deals with mythical, inhuman beings whom they, the pale merchants of Lorne or Suni, Arno, Yorque or Neo-Sirius, would never know. Their ultimate fear was that one day he would loom out of the sky over their cities at the head of a hostile fleet.

They feared him as sedentary merchants have always feared their captains because they did not know him. They could not fathom the source of his laughter or of his strength.

But it was because they were afraid of him that they trusted him. He was invincible; the holds of his ships were always fuller than anyone else's; and he was never defeated. The rewards were enormous, even in proportion to the risks.

And so, when the supreme magistrates of the sixteen cooperating planets interviewed other candidates, they were disappointed. This captain was too young, that one too timid. A good technician but a poor trader. Too rapacious. Too easy on his crew. Too tricky. Of doubtful courage. Health too much impaired by space diseases. Too old. Too unstable. Too mediocre.

Too something. The tall and handsome captains of the Lesser Magellanic Cloud filed past the supreme magistrates of the sixteen planets, but none was suitable. The assignment was too difficult for them and the stakes were too high. The magistrates hesitated. They did not want to lose the *Vasco*, the largest, most powerful manmade ship in this part of the universe.

Then Shangrin came in. He marched right up to them and said: "I'm taking the *Vasco*." He burst out laughing when he saw the expressions on their faces. As he looked over the handsome captains of the Lesser Magellanic Cloud he asked the supreme magistrates if they wanted children or a man.

He got the assignment and the *Vasco* was his. It meant, of course, new worries for the magistrates, new wrinkles, new ulcers, palpitations in their old hearts, but also—in the future—even greater prosperity. Along with the *Vasco*, they let him have an army of scientists, technicians, astronauts, soldiers.

And a mountain of recommendations.

They also gave him a first mate named Gregory, a reliable young man whose fame would perhaps some day equal Varun Shangrin's, and who might be able to bridle the captain's impetuousness.

Since they were a cautious lot, the supreme magistrates took an extra precaution: they made Gregory into a safety mechanism by secretly implanting strange devices in his mind. But as they were also discreet, they did not tell him. Nor Shangrin. Shangrin and Gregory plunged into intergalactic space with their ship and its crew, both yearning for conquest.

The *Vasco* and its crew were now on the way back to the Lesser Magellanic Cloud and the devices within Gregory had remained unused so far. They would have remained so if . . .

Shangrin was calmly raising his china tea cup when a sudden gesture of his first mate made him drop it. The tea spilled all over his red beard, the cup rolled on to his knees and shattered on the floor. Shangrin's blue eyes flashed. His heavy fists came down on the metal table, making it tremble.

"Have you no respect?" he shouted. "At least for this superb tea, if not for me?"

"The stars!" said Gregory.

"Well?"

The captain's eyes flew to the collection of screens which covered one wall of the room. His face, which had been flushed with anger, became ashen; his eyes bulged.

"The stars went off for a second, then came on again. But they're not the same ones! It all happened very quickly. If I hadn't happened to be looking at the screens at just that moment, I probably wouldn't have noticed anything. Except the new positions of the stars."

"Never saw anything like it."

Shangrin stood up, looking a lot like a bear. He leaned forward, hunched down, then suddenly he was erect, slightly stooped. He weighed two hundred and eighty pounds, was six feet six. Of his sixty-seven years, forty had been spent in outer space. He spoke with authority, was a good technician and a skilled trader.

He went to a screen which gave an excellent impression of transparency and depth.

"I don't know a single one of those constellations, not one. We must have made an enormous leap for the landscape to change that much. Look at the relative positions of the stars."

"Could the computers recognize any of those constellations and find our location?"

Captain Varnun Shangrin closed his eyes to think better and snapped his huge fingers two or three times. But no inspiration came.

"The astronauts and the passengers have noticed something, Captain," said Gregory. "They're beginning to worry."

Red lights were popping up everywhere. Almost all the posts on the ship wanted to communicate with the captain. Then the shrill ring of priority bells was heard. Shangrin did not stir.

"What are you looking for, Captain?"

Shangrin slowly looked up from under heavy lids.

"Something to say to them, young man. After all, we're lost, as far as I know. What I'm trying to figure out is how to make them think this is a bit of luck."

"That's a tough one."

"Over any length of time, impossible. But I can keep them quiet for ten minutes. Wait and see."

Shangrin ran his fingers along a keyboard. All the red lights went out; only one green light remained, the one for navigation.

"Cut all contact between Navigation and the rest of the ship," ordered Shangrin. "All private conversations are forbidden until further notice. All crew members will remain at their posts. They are not to answer questions from outside. Is that clear?"

"Yes," answered an anonymous voice.

Varun Shangrin cut the contact with a flick of his finger. Then he turned on the master switch.

Seconds later his voice echoed in all the corridors, public rooms, dining halls, dormitories and cabins of the *Vasco*.

"Captain Varun Shangrin speaking."

He cleared his throat and winked at Gregory.

"I have an announcement to make. First Mate Gregory and I have perfected an experiment which enables us to take a leap in time. We've just tried it out. That's the reason for the sudden change in the stellar horizon. We are going to take advantage of this side trip to visit a new region in space. This will not delay our return. Quite the contrary."

He disconnected the speaker.

"Is that the best you can do?" asked Gregory. "They'll be on our backs in an hour."

"A lot of things can happen in an hour. By then we may have no cause for worry. Or we may have found

out what happened. Or even—" he winked again—
"within the hour I may really have found the secret
of time leaps. Or you will."

"Neither of us is a technician, and I doubt if the
words 'time leap' mean anything."

"Frankly, I don't know," said Shangrin. "I realize
we're not scientists and that we couldn't possibly make
such a tremendous discovery. But we'll dream up some
story for them. That at least is within our power." He
gave his loud laugh.

"The essential, obviously, is that no one panic," admitted Gregory.

"Can't be done," said Shangrin. "It's bound to happen. There are already two people on board whose
insides are tied up in knots."

"Who?"

"You and me. Let's go see the navigators. Maybe
they know something."

"Okay," Gregory said hesitantly.

He knew how well his boss could bluff. He had seen
Shangrin talk his way out of tight spots hundreds of
times, spots others could not even have shot their way
out of. But that the captain would try to lie to the
Magellanites, his own people, was unthinkable.

The *Vasco*, however, had already done the unthinkable—it had gone beyond the stars.

Henrik, the bald little chief navigator, was jumping
up and down with surprise and fury.

"But it's illegal!" he protested. "You have no right
to forbid all communication between Navigation and
the rest of the ship. You cannot take away from the
crew the right to be kept informed. You should be—"

"Mr. Henrik," thundered Shangrin, "I have piloted
ships when the captain was the only one with any say-
so at all. Times have changed, I know, but I haven't.
Anyway, in unusual circumstances I am allowed to
assume full control. Now let's get down to business.
Every minute counts."

Swallowing his rage, Henrik led them into the control

room. It was spherical, surrounded by limitless space. The walls were invisible. Stars shone in the dark. Sometimes larger spots would loom up: nebulous, distant little islands of stars; sometimes a nova, like a lighthouse set up to guide navigators in a billion-chambered labyrinth of the universe.

The vast cabin where the navigators operated floated in the center of the sphere, reached by a light, transparent gangplank. Henrik, Shangrin and Gregory climbed up.

The visible space was an artificial creation. Stars were not directly visible in the second continuum, in which the *Vasco* was traveling at a speed greater than that of light. Furthermore, normal space in this continuum was subject to transformations which altered the relationships between distances. For this reason, complex instruments reconstructed on the wall of the sphere an image of space such as might have been seen by a hypothetical traveler going through space on the same trajectory and at the same speed as the *Vasco*.

The navigation room was a superb and costly equipment center. Its usefulness during long cruises was questionable, for the overall operation was performed automatically by computers. But the Magellanites liked it because they preferred human control to mechanical control. It gave them, in stellar clusters, a maneuverability that was envied even by the pilots of Prime-Galaxy who had better, more sensitive, but still automatic instruments.

"Where are we?" Gregory asked under his breath, as though speaking to himself. "I don't recognize anything in the position of the stars."

Henrik raised his arms.

"I don't either. Nothing is familiar. Nothing. Absolutely nothing. And I know this sector like the palm of my hand. The sector we were cruising in before this accident, that is. We'll never find our way again. Never."

"If I hear you say that again," roared Shangrin, "I'll

wring your neck and throw you out into space. We'll get out of here and with something to show for it."

"All right, Captain," Henrik replied with obvious restraint.

"What do the integrators show?"

"Nothing yet. I put them into operation at once. I thought at first that we'd taken a huge jump into second space for some unknown reason and that we didn't recognize the stars anymore because the perspective had changed. I have the integrators systematically comparing the positions of the stars that can be observed with the information available in our atlases. But up to now, they haven't identified a single constellation."

"I see. Topological analysis. And no nova, no known nebula?"

"Nothing in the way of novae. The integrators don't function on nebulae. Only on stars that are relatively close. Incidentally, have you noticed anything?"

"The stars here are clearly more numerous than in the space we have just left," Gregory said.

"Right. We were just crossing the chasm separating the Lesser Magellanic Cloud from the Greater, where stars are relatively rare. Here, they are distributed more densely. Much as in a local cluster of small size."

"I see," said Shangrin. "And there will be a definite answer from the integrators in . . . ?"

"Maybe one minute. Maybe never. Of course we can ask them for an approximate answer any time now."

"Go ahead," said Shangrin.

Henrik gave some orders. The men bending over their control panels got busy. The voice of the computer could be heard, muffled, throbbing.

". . . There is no system of stars consisting of more than twelve units corresponding, within a frame of point zero five, with any known structure. In about twelve hours it will be possible to determine the general outline of the stellar cluster surrounding us. However, first calculations indicate that its shape is quite different from the one we have just left. However, three distant galaxies have been observed: these could be, respectively, the Prime-Galaxy, Andromeda's Nebula and the Swan Cluster. It should, however, be noted that they seem to be markedly nearer than they ought to be according to our atlases and that their light—"

"Shut it off," roared Shangrin.

Henrik gave a signal. The computer stopped intoning.

"Of course I don't believe a word of your time leap. It's nothing but a lie."

"I know," said Shangrin. "So what? I tried to preserve the calm and I've succeeded for the time being. What did you expect me to tell them?"

"The truth."

'In other words, that we are lost and we'll probably never see our own worlds again?"

"Maybe."

"You think that would have made them more likely to forgive me?"

"I don't know," said Henrik. "But I know you're finished. The committee will fire you."

"You'd like that, wouldn't you? But you'll have to wait a while. This being an emergency, I'm taking over. I'll dissolve the committee if I have to."

Henrik choked.

"You can't push us around. The guardians will take steps."

"I'm not afraid of the guardians."

Henrik flailed at the air with his thin arms as though he were struggling for breath. Gregory dragged the captain out.

CHAPTER II

"You have a terrible disposition, Captain," Gregory said cautiously, feeling as though he were walking on thin ice.

Shangrin did not answer. There were little drops of sweat on his forehead. He could be silent for hours on end; for as long as his anger lasted.

Gregory thought hard. The situation was serious—physically and psychologically. Physically, it had not yet become critical. True, they were lost in an unknown universe, but the *Vasco* had enough supplies to continue its cruise for ten, twenty, a hundred years. Psychologically, however, a crisis loomed. People wouldn't like to be on a trip that went nowhere. The captain was sure to be dismissed within a matter of hours. He would put up a fight, of course, and his admirers would find excuses for all his tricks, all his bluffs. They would follow him, if need be, to the ends of the universe. But he also had enemies who did not care for his high-handed ways. A struggle would certainly ensue between the two factions. The unavoidable close quarters, even on a ship the size of the *Vasco*, tended more to fan enmities than to bind friendships.

If Shangrin were to resist the council, the guardians would intervene—but that was the unknown. It was general knowledge that on all ships there were guardians in charge of maintaining order in an emergency, in accordance with the laws of the Lesser Magellanic Cloud. But no one seemed to have any information about them. Were they agents on board or were they cybernators equipped to do police work? Rumor had it that the guardians were nothing but a myth made up

16

to intimidate the crew, keeping them from mutiny, and the captain, compelling him to obey the council and the laws.

Gregory reminded himself that the captain had deliberately precipitated the crisis. With his tale of a time leap, he had knowingly unleashed a wave of anger which would lead to his dismissal by the council. He must have foreseen this. He was stubborn, short-tempered, impulsive and arrogant, but he was also intelligent. Why had he stuck his neck out? For a few minutes of peace? Nonsense. Does one use nuclear weapons to squash a fly?

Gregory stared at the screens. They showed a landscape similar to hundreds of millions of others he'd seen. Why did they seem strange? What was the distance between these stars and the Lesser Magellanic Cloud, with its prosperous cities, its ships, its factories, its museums, its women? The thickness of a universe? The infinite?

The instruments quietly went on with their work, observing, translating, noting, remembering, recording, in a whirlwind of infinitesimal flashes, sealed into the irregularities of a piece of crystal. Date and place mattered little to them. It did to men. After traveling for twelve years, they were looking forward to coming back to the welcoming ports of the Lesser Magellanics and enjoying their share of the rich booty of the expedition. Instead of that, they were being offered a new lease on space.

Why had Shangrin spoken of instant propulsion, Gregory wondered, and why had he put himself in the limelight? Because he thought that instant propulsion was the only possible explanation for what had actually happened to the *Vasco?* Most unlikely. He could just as easily have intimated that the ship had fallen into an air pocket, and could have added the comforting thought that they could reverse direction. This would have been the easiest, most obvious explanation for the accident.

Gregory looked at the captain out of the corner of

his eye. Shangrin, his eyes closed, appeared to be asleep. But he was thinking, fast and hard. It was always when he seemed relaxed, free from any tension, at complete ease, that he was at his most dangerous.

He must have some idea in the back of his mind, Gregory decided. Perhaps he believed that somebody on board the *Vasco* actually knew the secret of instant propulsion and had tried to use it. Then that somebody could easily straighten things and Captain Varun Shangrin's reputation would be undamaged. Shangrin had acted, Gregory thought, as though he were trying to cover up for someone.

Who could it be? A member of the crew? One of the physicists? One of the mathematicians? One of the psychomaticians who juggled in most alarming ways with the capacities of the nervous system? No. Shangrin would not have thought twice about denouncing any of them. And anyway, why would a member of the crew have conducted an experiment of such magnitude in the most complete secrecy?

There was only one person on board the *Vasco* both capable of successfully conducting so surprising an attempt and whom the captain might want to protect. A shiver ran up and down Gregory's back. His neck became tense. Not really a person—a being, at most. The Runi.

Gregory tried to keep his hands from shaking. The Runi. That explained everything, or almost everything. The pieces of the puzzle fell into place easily now. Who except the Runi would wish to head the ship in the opposite direction from the Lesser Magellanics? Who would possibly have the power to do it if not the Runi? And the Runi's presence on board was something the captain was very anxious to hide.

Gregory had not thought of the Runi before because he just had not believed that so monstrous a creature could have such a range of scientific knowledge. He remembered the night when he and the captain had smuggled the Runi on board, in flagrant violation of the rules. It had been a strange experience to enter the ship under their command like thieves, to hoodwink the sentries and deactivate the alarms. Shangrin's reasons for introducing the Runi on board had always seemed obscure. But the captain seemed to care more for his monster than for his share of the loot. Was it because the Runi seemed to enjoy their games of chess as much as Shangrin did? Or because he seemed to be the repository of a considerable body of scientific knowledge which Shangrin was hoping to put to use? But how could one know, with that sort of creature, if one was merely being made use of?

Gregory made a face. He had pretty unpleasant memories of the Runi's planet. The xenologists had decided that the Runis were feebleminded and everyone except Shangrin had taken their word for it. Shangrin had persisted in teaching one of them to play chess. The chessboard, with its sixty-four squares, had served to bridge the gap between the mental universes of the Runis and the humans. The xenologists had eventually revised their concepts and perfected a translation apparatus. Incoherent shreds of the Runis' knowledge had come through.

Very few of these had any parallels in human knowledge; only a few seemed to possess even a shadow of meaning. The question of how the Runis had penetrated certain secrets of the universe had remained unanswered. They had no apparent civilization, no language, no technology, no instruments. They seemed content to set up rows of pebbles or twigs in apparently meaningless arrangements on the yellow plains of their planet. Then they would leave. A long time later, possibly, a Runi would pass by, touch up a detail and continue on his way.

It was like a series of endless games, which was what had given Shangrin the idea of teaching them chess.

Gregory took two steps toward the captain and touched his shoulder.

"The Runi," he said.

Shangrin growled and opened his eyes.

"You believe we owe this side trip to the Runi," Gregory said accusingly.

"Yes," admitted Shangrin.

"But he has no instruments, no source of energy, no—"

"They can do things we can't even imagine," said Shangrin in a slow, tired voice.

"And you think you can make him put us back on our trajectory?"

"If I can still beat him at chess, yes."

There was a note of despair in Shangrin's voice. Gregory knew that the Runi made tremendous progress with each game. At first, Shangrin could easily beat him just by thinking; the last few games he had played with the aid of a computer. And Shangrin had fifty years of experience behind him. The Runi had a phenomenal memory and his logic was flawless; very soon he would be better than any human. He was not very quick—time was of no consequence on his planet—but it was not important for chess players either. Some games went on for months, years.

"Why don't we go see him?"

"I was getting ready to," said Shangrin. "I was thinking out Eichenhorn's gambit."

Gregory knew how the chess pieces moved, although he did not share the captain's passion. He preferred faster moving, more intense games in which the opponent's personality was revealed more directly.

Shangrin got up heavily; his bearlike figure showed fatigue.

"You think it's my fault, don't you, that I saw a gold mine in the Runi?"

Gregory did not reply.

"You're right, but not altogether. I've been traveling in space for a long time and it's given me a couple of ideas. The chief one is that man's expansion in the universe is a miracle. Incredible and fragile. Thirty or forty thousand years ago—I'm a little vague—they lived on only one planet in the Prime-Galaxy, which they called the Milky Way. During that time they secured a foothold on three or four galaxies. We ourselves are only an outer limb, easily detachable from the parent tree.

"And men, as they conquered the stars, had many setbacks, but there was never any serious question about their power. It's a miracle, I tell you, Gregory. Incredible luck. Sooner or later, it will come to an end. No one can win all the time.

"Sooner or later, something will happen. A cataclysm. A meeting with another species more powerful, just as domineering. It will never be more than a slight hitch in the history of the universe, but for mankind it will be the end.

"Of course, if we could bring another race into play, it would be quite a trump card. The Runis represent one more chance. Whatever they know, whatever they can do over and beyond what we know and are capable of, almost constitutes that trump. It could also raise our capabilities to the level of our ambitions. But there is an element of risk: some day the Runis may turn against us, or drop us at a crucial point. I accepted his coming with us. Perhaps that was a mistake."

"You've never talked to me like this," said Gregory.

"What good would it have done? This is such a solemn speech that it sounds hollow. Personally, I like reality, things that are concrete, clear. Most people think of me as nothing but a brute in space. They're right. I like money and power. I am overbearing and my ideas belong to another generation. But that doesn't keep me from being farsighted."

He put a huge hand on Gregory's shoulder, about a head lower than his own.

"You're a different breed. You're not afraid of the gods, nor fate, nor space. Perhaps that will come with age. I can't remember how I felt at your age. But if you give in to this fear, then you'll make mistakes too."

His hand dropped and he stroked his beard pensively.

"Let's go ask the Runi what he thinks."

Is he sincere? Gregory wondered. It was impossible to tell. If the old captain had been trying to get at him through his better self, he certainly had almost succeeded.

CHAPTER III

The Runi occupied a stateroom cluttered with a mass of paraphernalia designed for his survival and communication with humans. He looked like a furry crab. An orange shell protected that part of his nervous system which was encased in a fur-covered cylinder. The cylinder was made up of seven rings of approximately the same diameter as a human body. The Runi could stretch his length to four yards or compress his rings to less than one. He rested by coiling up. There were about a dozen small, articulated limbs where the body and the shell joined. They looked like surgical instruments and served as sense organs, fingers and tools.

The Runi, coiled up on the floor, looked like a crab resting on a huge ball of wool. Next to him there was a chessboard. His body was a prisoner of the instruments for communication.

When the two men came in, the Runi quivered and the instruments tried to interpret this in human language.

"Goodnessgoodnessgoodnessgoodness when will you take me back to my planet goodnessgoodnessgoodness goodness."

"That's enough of that," Shangrin said curtly.

He put his hands in his pockets and considered his passenger. The Runi's little organs were quivering—a repellent sight.

"Enoughenoughenoughenoughenough," the Runi started up.

He stretched out slightly. A shiver ran over his orange fur. He's completely stupid, Gregory said to himself. The xenologists were right. I don't know why

Shangrin persists in thinking these beasts have any intelligence.

"Listen, Runi," said Shangrin. "You admit that I beat you fairly?"

"Truetruetruetruetrue," said the Runi.

"Okay. And you accepted the terms of the deal we made. If you win, I am to stay for 10 years on your planet to improve your chess playing. If I win, you are to spend ten years on my planet. In any event, the deal is to your advantage because I don't expect to live more than one hundred and fifty years, whereas two or three millennia are nothing to you."

"Truetruetruetruetruetrue."

"Damn it," said Shangrin. "The interpreting system has broken down again."

He leaned over the instruments and checked their wires. He made a delicate adjustment.

"There. I think that will stop the stuttering."

So it was the machine's fault, Gregory thought. He ought to have worked it out for himself. When so vast a chasm separated two species that they had to depend upon a mechanical bridge to close it, they had to be convinced that their mutual misunderstandings stemmed solely from the machines. Perhaps the xenologists' mistake had been too blind a trust in their instruments. But how could one ever know what the other was thinking then? The machine could always introduce something extraneous into the message. It could be no more than a shade of meaning, but in the long run the whole message could be based on false data. Semantics now involved more than just words, but attitudes, infinitesimal movements of articulated members and vibrations of hairs, so how could one ever be sure of what the other was trying to convey?

Instruments were no longer sufficient. Intuition was needed, good old-fashioned, reliable intuition of the Varun Shangrin kind.

"You haven't stuck to the deal," said Shangrin. "You tried to cheat, Runi. You've set off a mechanism that I don't know so that you can go home to your planet in this continuum. You've no right to do this. You're going to take us back to where you made us turn off, Runi."

How can a non-human have any sense of honor? Gregory wondered. Has he any concept of honesty? Friendship? Suffering? Can these be contained in the somewhat unusual guise of a furry crab?

The body stretched out to almost its full length; the orange carapace balanced on the fur-covered cylinder. The articulated paws were wriggling frenetically.

"That's not true, not true," answered the machine. "We are lost, lost, lost . . ."

Silence followed. Then the machine interpreted in a louder and clearer voice.

"That's not true. We are lost in the continuum. But it's not my fault. Runis can't do anything like that."

A blue vein on Shangrin's left temple began to throb.

"Where are we, Runi?" he shouted.

The Runi's head almost reached the man's. Thousands of threads, finer than hair, connected it to the interpreting machines and formed a sort of metal halo around it.

It can't be, thought Gregory. He has no way of locating us in space. He has no instruments, not even a radio telescope, not even a screen on which he can see the stars.

But the answer came very quickly.

"We're still in the same place," said the Runi, "taking into account the movement of the ship. We are not in a different sector of space, nor with noticeably different coordinates in space."

"That can't be, Runi," said Shangrin. We don't know any of those stars. We can't find a single familiar constellation. Even the galaxies are different. You're lying, Runi."

"Nonononononono, I'm not lying. I don't know what happened. Something caused a change in the environment. The mass ate up time. Inertia is perpendicular to the ray's phase. C has increased. I repeat, C has increased."

"The machine is off the track," said Gregory," or else the Runi is."

"I don't think so," said Shangrin. "The Runi wants to tell us something, but the machine isn't really programmed to express it. The Runi says more in one second than you could in a month, but the machine translates only what makes sense to it. We must appear feebleminded to the Runi. The questions we ask him are deplorably simple."

But he plays chess slowly, Gregory thought. Then the answer came to him in a flash. It's because he explores all the possibilities and because he probably starts—simultaneously—a number of other operations we know nothing about.

"It's not a leap in space," the Runi went on, "but a leap in time. As I understand it, the sines are disassociated in your consciousness. Your ship has taken a leap backward. Into the past. A leap of two hundred million of your years."

"The machine is on the blink again," said Gregory. Shangrin shot him a disgusted look.

"Quiet. Can't you see he's telling the truth?"

Gregory began to tremble.

"But he can't be."

"I can prove it," the Runi went on steadily. "The inertia of a mass depends upon the age of the universe. It decreases with time. It has suddenly increased. Your instruments must have registered it."

There was a shade of pity in the Runi's speech. Or had the translating machine added it? It was impossible to tell.

"The universe, considered as a closed system, loses some of its mass as it grows old," the Runi went on. "This phenomenon can be looked upon as an effect of expansion, or, conversely, the expansion can be looked upon as an approximate expression of that process. Time consumes mass. It would seem that the relationship is reversible. Mass has consumed time. I have no means of telling whether the incident has an artificial cause. Somewhere there might be an entity that controls time and that has projected the ship into a distant past. If my supposition is correct, this entity cannot be beaten in chess. Indeed, the game can be of no interest to it."

The Runi's last statement seemed a non sequitur. But it wasn't, Gregory said to himself. Before the arrival of the *Vasco* on their planet, the Runis had probably never suspected that there could be another thinking species in the universe. Then the game of chess had seemed to them to be the necessary intermediary between two thinking species. It was, therefore, an enormously important tool.

It all pointed to one thing: the Runi knew the humans infinitely better than they understood him. And, for the first time, they were dependent upon him. That might give him ideas.

"Two hundred million years," said Shangrin, blinking.

He turned to the Runi.

"Is there some way of getting back to our time?"

"I don't see any," said the Runi. "I'm not equipped to understand the problems of time. I merely noticed that we had passed, with no transition, from one state of the universe to another. If our displacement was the result of the will of a living being, he surely can put us back into our time."

"How can we make contact with this . . . entity?"

"I don't know," replied the Runi. "But I want you to understand one thing. Even though our worlds are relatively far apart in space, they are neighbors in time. At the period where we now are, neither your race nor mine was yet in existence. I'm just as lost as you are. I want, just as you do, to get back to my planet and to my mate. The force of circumstances is making me your ally."

Shangrin seemed to be deeply moved.

"We see eye to eye, Runi," he said in a deep voice. "We'll get out of this together. What are you going to do? Do you need anything?"

The Runi resumed his resting position. Slow undulations ran up and down the fur on his orange rings.

"No," said the translating machine. "I'm going to go back to studying the moves of the knight."

Shangrin appeared to have lost the game. But Gregory saw that he was smiling.

"It's going to be a tough fight," said the captain.

And Gregory wondered if Shangrin was referring to the confrontation with time, the unknown entity, or the crew of the *Vasco*.

CHAPTER IV

The robot-usher was going down the concentric corridors of the *Vasco*. He was dressed traditionally in black. There was a little gold scale suspended on his chest from a gold chain. When he was wearing that symbol, the humans had to obey his orders. More rarely, a small gold sword swung on his black thorax, showing his authorization to use force.

He always followed a well-defined itinerary on his way to meet someone who was not expecting him. He entered an imitation park. The robot-gardeners had completely transformed it during the night, doing away with the lake, creating a river, setting up hills and planting trees. They had also changed the artificial color of the sky and chosen a nostalgic shade with grayish tones. The grass was green, tall and prickly. There were flowers scattered on the slopes. The robot-gardeners changed the imitation parks as often as possible to keep the humans from getting bored with familiar landscapes. They undertook these transformations at irregular intervals and without warning, so that when the humans went to the park, they never knew what they were going to find. That was apparently enough to keep them happy.

The robot-usher knew all this, but it was a matter of complete indifference to him. He even knew that the name of this particular setup was the Prime-Galaxy. For him, the Prime-Galaxy was only a fabulously distant cluster of stars and the source for a large part of the regulations he was supposed to enforce. He was just capable of realizing that the Prime-Galaxy must have consisted of a large number of worlds and that they

29

probably did not all look like this landscape. On the other hand he was totally unaware that the hills, the river, the grass and the trees corresponded to the mythical image of a specific world which had been the cradle of the human species.

And yet he was aware of the odd and exotic qualities of the landscape.

The humans were equally aware of it, for they strolled about in it, giving little exclamations of surprise. Some of them were already stretched out on the grass. A group of children played on the river bank, supervised by a human teacher. The robot-usher disapproved of human educators. He thought this a work task unworthy of humans. Indeed, he considered all work unworthy of humans. He saw in the presence of the teachers the regrettable influence of modern ideas.

He walked resolutely toward the teacher, leaving no trace in the grass for the excellent reason that he glided along in the air a few centimeters above the ground.

He eyed the supervisor closely. Blonde, thirty years old. Blue trousers and blouse. Tanned oval face. Very light blue eyes.

She was smiling peacefully and seemed very sure of herself.

The robot-usher rose a little and went up to her. He was not really supposed to dominate over humans in this way, but he thought it was more dignified and this increase in dignity would be automatically reflected on humans. He was an expert at rationalizing.

"Norma Shundi?" he asked.

She turned quickly.

"What do you want?"

"You've been asked to attend the meeting. It will start at eight P.M. The business is a request for the dismissal of Captain Shangrin."

She gave a start.

"Dismiss the captain? Why?"

"The request cites an alleged overstepping of authority."

"Oh, that. I don't even know what happened. Wait a minute. Are the charges only against the captain?"

"The second in command is automatically implicated."

"Gregory, oh Gregory," she said with the hint of a sob in her voice. "I can't preside."

"You haven't any choice. You're not sick. You have no valid reason to refuse."

"I've never attended; I don't know how."

"Most of the members who are to be there tonight are no more experienced than you."

"Isn't there a way out?"

"None," said the robot.

"But it's absurd to pick people out at random."

"That's the rule."

The usher turned on his heel and left. It was strange how differently people reacted when he brought them word that they were to preside. Some were plainly flattered. Others, on the contrary, seemed to be afraid they weren't up to it. Only a few showed complete indifference, but even they came to the meetings. There were penalties for staying away without valid reasons, although these seldom had to be applied. His small gold sword with its chain remained, more often than not, in a drawer.

He had five more humans to see. The list had been drawn up by the statistical service in charge of membership. The members were simply drawn by lot from among the adults on board the *Vasco*. This democratic system prevailed on all ships of the Lesser Magellanic Clouds, as the final outgrowth of public-opinion polls. It had been common knowledge for a long time that one could know the opinions and wishes of a great many people by questioning only a small segment of the population. The next step had been to invest power in that small segment. The council on board the *Vasco* met at irregular intervals, whenever there was an important problem, at the request of the captain or of a given number of passengers. Anyone was liable to be selected—anyone except a handful of specialists whose impartiality was considered essential, such as members of the fighting squadrons.

The difficulty inherent in such a system was keeping any one person from controlling the composition of the council. This was one of the responsibilities of the robot-ushers.

Norma Shundi looked for Gregory as she entered the Council Hall. The platform was still empty. The charges were summed up on a lighted board: abuse of power, which could endanger the ship and its passengers.

The request for dismissal was anonymous, as prescribed.

Who dared? she wondered.

She settled herself into an armchair and looked up at the black ceiling on which could be seen the milky and irregular trail of the Magellanic Nebula. Where are we in space? she asked herself. There were rumors afoot than an accident had pushed them off their course, but she was unconcerned. She was rather happy on the *Vasco*: she liked looking after children and she particularly liked Gregory.

She saw that Henrik, the chief navigator, was making an ostentatious entrance into his box. The robot-ushers finally arrived and the hall began to fill quickly. One of her colleagues, a silent, withdrawn young man, sat down next to her.

One of the ushers made a few stock pronouncements and formally declared the meeting open. Only then did Varun Shangrin sit down at the raised platform. Gregory followed close behind. There was total silence for one full minute. Norma scanned Shangrin's face, then Gregory's. The captain towered over the council; Gregory looked almost puny next to him.

A murmur of voices rose. Shangrin did not move. There were stacks of documents on Henrik's desk and he checked through them feverishly. From time to time he darted an anxious look at Shangrin.

The captain stroked his red beard.

"I want the floor," he thundered.

The murmuring died down, then a sudden silence settled on the assembly.

"And I'm taking it," he said in a quieter voice. "So, some of you thought you could take advantage of the situation and demand my dismissal. Unfortunately, that will not be possible."

He looked around at his audience.

"I have just resigned."

One of the men on the council stood up.

"We cannot under present circumstances, accept it," he said. 'We want some details first."

"Yes, yes," came a chorus of voices. "We want to know what happened."

Gregory was smiling. He can't be worried, Norma said to herself. He must have something up his sleeve.

"What do you think happened?" Shangrin asked the man who was objecting. An usher intervened.

"The questioner must identify himself."

"Peer Nardi," said the man, "xenologist." He was tall and slender and his iron gray hair gave him an air of distinction. He spoke clearly and somewhat sharply.

"I've heard a great many rumors today," he went on. "It seems that for some unknown reason the ship made an enormous leap in space and that we are now in parts unknown. On the other hand, Captain, I heard your claim that a method of instant propulsion had been discovered, and that you had conducted an experiment. I confess it hard to believe in such a discovery. I don't like these nebulous claims. What is being kept from us?"

Another man got up. Norma knew him by sight. He lived in the same section as she did, and often seemed to watch her admiringly.

"Jal Derin," he said, "metrologist. My field is precision instruments. I've noticed certain abberations. I tried to get in touch with the physics section of navigation to find out whether something similar had been observed. But I couldn't get through. This is an outrage."

He looked put out.

Henrik began to stir behind his table.

"I had orders."

"Orders from whom?"

"The captain."

"Have you any idea where we are?"

Henrik hesitated.

"Yes, but it's so fantastic that—"

"I order you to keep quiet," shouted Shangrin, standing and looking menacing. He gave the impression of intending to strangle Henrik if the latter spoke.

"No," shouted everyone.

Shangrin ignored the shouts.

"Is that all?"

"No," said a woman. "Dora Norte, biologist. There is a rumor that our trip will last at least ten more years, possibly more, before we get back to the Lesser Magellanics. Is that true?"

"I don't know, ma'am," Shangrin replied in a voice that had sudenly become honeyed. "Personally, I should be happy to travel in your company for another ten years."

There was laughter, quickly smothered. He's clowning, Norma said to herself. Is that his only trump, to gain time by playing to the gallery?

"I protest the silencing of Henrik," Jal Derin said.

"Objection overruled," a robot-usher said calmly.

"Henrik can speak later for as long as he wants," thundered Shangrin. "But he'll have to wait his turn. Right now I'm going to tell you what happened."

Silence followed. The two men and the woman sat down again.

"It happened at seven thirty-eight," the huge man began. "Without any warning, the sky changed. Anyone looking at a screen could see this . . ."

On the screen behind him, the text of the charges against him vanished and space, as it was now visible from the fore of the *Vasco*, came on.

"We were lost. I didn't recognize a single one of the visible constellations. I had to give Navigation time to try to establish our position. I wanted to avoid a panic.

I forbade all communication between Navigation and the rest of the ship. I announced that *I* was in sole control."

He took a deep breath.

"It wasn't true."

He paused, but no one spoke. His trump card was the unvarnished truth.

"I thought that we could speedily determine the causes of the phenomenon and that we could then straighten everything out. But it was impossible."

Voices rose.

"Resign! Resign!"

"I have."

The robot-ushers flitted about the hall to reestablish silence.

"I studied those stars carefully," said Shangrin. "And an idea came to me. I asked Henrik, in Navigation, to try an experiment."

Henrik stood up.

"It's fantastic," he said. "With the help of the computers, I—"

Shangrin interrupted.

"Show us the map of the sky I asked you to make up."

"But . . ."

"Go on. You can talk later."

A screen which had been blank until then was lit up above the one that showed the present view. Stars shone in a blank sky. A quick comparison was possible. There were great differences, but the general disposition of the constellations was the same. In the chart below a few luminous points showed as novae which were missing from the one above.

"This map," said Shangrin pointing to the original, lower screen, "shows a section of the sky actually around us now."

He gave a signal and a third screen at the top of the wall was lit up.

"This one shows the *Vasco's* horizon before the phenomenon."

His voice became dramatic. He raised his head and pointed his beard toward the members of the council.

"The middle one is the result of Henrik's labors. It is something quite special. It represents the same region of the sky as the one above, but with one difference. It shows the state of that region of the sky as it was *two hundred million years ago.*"

He gave a crushing smile.

"As a matter of fact, a little more: between two hundred and fifteen and two hundred and thirty million years, to be precise. Your turn, Henrik."

Henrik shuffled his papers frantically. His bald pate reflected the light. His agitation was caused more by the discovery than by fear.

"The similarity between this chart and the portion of the sky actually before us is striking. There are numerous details missing which correspond to cataclysms that left no trace. But, in general, the constellations correspond."

"Which means," said Shangrin, "that we have not traveled in space but in time—a leap of two hundred million years into the past. We are still headed toward the Lesser Magellanic Cloud, but it now looks the way it did long before it was settled by man. In fact, the way it looked two hundred million years ago. We've jumped squarely into the past."

"Dear God!" a woman's voice whispered.

"We'll never see home again. You must get that firmly in your minds before you come to any decision." He added quickly, "The meeting is recessed for twenty minutes. The members of the committee may not communicate with anyone else on board during the recess."

He turned on his heel and left the hall. Gregory followed. Voices rose but fell almost at once, as small groups quietly started to discuss what Shangrin had told them.

This can't be happening; it's incredible, thought Norma as she headed toward the corridor. The ship seemed so real, so calm. Nothing had changed. There were a few lights in the sky that had barely moved. Two hundred million years! She didn't feel one second younger. The stars said that the universe which contained them was two hundred million years younger than the one in which they had been born—surely the stars were lying. She stopped at the threshold of the captain's minute office. Gregory's back was turned to her. He was sitting in front of a screen that showed a picture of the sky. There were seven luminous dots slowly moving amid the stars. She moved up silently and placed her hands on Gregory's shoulders.

He flicked off the light on the screen.

"Norma," he said without looking around.

"He's next door?"

He indicated with his chin the door of the control room.

"That was quite a performance he gave. You too," she said.

"I didn't say anything."

"That doesn't matter. You seemed so sure of yourself."

"It was just an illusion."

"They won't fire him, will they?"

"I don't know."

He got up and took her in his arms. But his mind was elsewhere.

"You shouldn't have come," he said.

"I know, but I had to tell you that it makes no difference to me if I never see Suni or Lorne or any of our other planets again. As long as you're here, I don't care."

"We can't live on this ship forever. We'll have to land somewhere."

"And there is no human being anywhere in the universe except us? I don't care."

"That's not what I meant. Anyway . . ."

"Anyway?"

"Nothing. You'll find out later."

She didn't insist. She snuggled closer to him, but he gently pushed her away.

"Not now."

Disappointed, she pulled back.

"Will he actually resign? I really hope so—then you could be free."

"You're crazy," he said. "Anyway, I don't know what he's going to do. No one ever knows what he's thinking, but, no, I think he likes power too much to resign."

"He's playing with them," she said. "I'd like him to be fired, but at the same time I'd like him to succeed."

"He knows how to manipulate people, all right," he admitted, "but it's a close thing."

"Are things as bad as he says?"

"Worse."

'I don't believe it."

The shrill ringing of the bell announcing the end of the recess could be heard down the corridors, echoing on the metal walls. They heard Shangrin's grumble, and then his heavy tread, behind the door.

"I'll see you tonight," she said from the hall.

The three screens behind the platform were dark. Henrik, gnome-like, was struggling with a barrage of questions. The council members were beginning to take in the full impact of recent events. They were thinking that they too would soon have to field worried questions. The truth would spread like wind in the great ship. It would blow through the living quarters, the imitation parks, the recreation centers, the factories, the laboratories. It would run along waves and wires to reach the ship's periphery; the scouting craft and observation posts. It would be whispered, shouted, printed, read. In an hour or two, the ship's sphere would be nothing but a ball of worry rolling along the unknown depths of the past.

"You've had time to think about our situation," Shangrin said. "Are there any questions?"

At first, no one stirred, then a man who was almost as old and massive as Shangrin stood up.

"Arno Linz, warrant officer. Do you know the reason for the phenomenon?"

Everyone knew Linz. He had been in charge of the first exploration boat to land on the planet of the Runis. He was a hard, pitiless man, a loner with a long background of adventures. He had explored more worlds than anyone on the *Vasco*. He had also collected more scars than anyone else.

"I don't know," said Shangrin. "And yet . . ." He stroked his beard and paused for a moment. "I've thought a great deal about it and I don't believe the catastrophe was brought on by natural causes."

"The phenomenon was induced?"

"I believe that a voyage in time constitutes a violation of physical laws. I think it's an artificial phenomenon."

General hubbub.

"Induced by someone on the *Vasco*?"

"That's not what I said. I think it's an external act of aggression."

The noise doubled in volume. Norma gripped the arms of her chair so hard that her knuckles hurt. Henrik stood up and pointed an accusatory finger at Shangrin.

"Where did you get that idea?"

"I've been thinking."

"Listen, Shangrin, you've got some pretty peculiar ideas right now. And peculiarly accurate ones. Whose idea was it to ask me for a chart of the sky as it was two hundred million years ago?"

"A pixie's."

"I'm not questioning your intelligence, but not one of us thought of a leap into the past. It was totally illogical. It's not the sort of idea that just comes. Where did you get it?"

"No comment."

Peer Nardi stood up.

"Varun Shangrin," he said, "I demand that you, as captain of this ship, give an answer. You have no right to keep to yourself a piece of information that concerns us all. You speak of aggression. You seem to know a lot about what has occurred. I accuse you of complicity with the aggressor."

Silence.

"I've spoken of the possibility of aggression," said Shangrin, "and I think it's our best bet."

"Why?"

"Because an aggressor can be forced to repair the damage he has caused."

He was so majestic, so Olympian, that Norma relaxed, leaned back in her chair and closed her eyes. Were they really at war? Wasn't it bad enough to be lost in the depths of the past?

"Frankly, I'm not sure of anything," said Shangrin. "But, right now, we may be in possession of a part of the answer."

A screen was lit up. Seven luminous dots in regular formation moved about against a background of stars.

"These are ships. The method of propulsion is primitive, probably inadequate for long interstellar runs. These ships are visible in a ray of a few light-years. And they were built some two hundred thousand years before man had left the planet of his birth."

The committee members were riveted, perhaps with fear, or perhaps they realized the drama of that instant. Norma could not make up her mind.

"These craft were spotted less than an hour ago by Detection. They are flying toward us, but we are not their target."

He was looking at her, Norma thought. He was staring at her with those enormous, almost globular, china-blue eyes. Did he know about her and Gregory? He would have disapproved. He had high hopes for Gregory and he insisted that a leader must be alone.

"I would like to ask Zoltan, our distinguished biologist, a question," Shangrin threw out. "How old is the human species?"

The biologist got up. He was a young man with a disproportionately high forehead. He was so thin that he was ugly. His hands were never still; they ran up and down his shirt like yellowish spiders.

"About one million years."

"Could there have been one or several other species before that?"

The biologist shook his head.

"It's a moot question. During the course of their expansion in the universe, men have occasionally come across similar or humanoid species. Give or take a few million years, they are not very much more ancient than man himself."

"And other species?"

"Officially, yes. We know of traces of life that are at least five billion years old."

"Thinking life?"

"We don't know. I don't think so, but there may well have been civilizations more than a billion years ago."

"So that we could run into a non-human civilization?"

"Yes, I think that's at least possible."

The biologist's hands betrayed his uncertainty. He blinked. He couldn't see what Shangrin was getting at.

"And a human civilization?"

"No, positively not. The most valid theory to account for the appearance of various similar species, outside of the one of common origin, postulates that forms of life succeed one another in great waves which correspond, each one, to a well defined stage of development of the universe. We belong to the carbon cycle; all the species of this cycle appeared more or less simultaneously and generally followed the same stages of evolution. It leads to man. Perhaps beyond him."

Shangrin then addressed the members of the council.

"Zoltan is one of the finest biologists of the Lesser Magellanics, the man who developed the concept of biological eras, of vital patterns that succeed one another in the universe like waves. He says that those ships cannot possibly be piloted by humans."

"I didn't say that," protested Zoltan. "I only said

that it is my belief that man has not yet made his appearance in the universe."

"Very well, we'll ask the opinion of the head of the Xenology Department, Smirno."

A murmur ran through the council. Smirno was Shangrin's most determined opponent, almost a personal enemy. Their fight over the Runis had made the *Vasco* tremble. The xenologist's box had remained empty during the first part of the meeting. The council members had assumed his absence was caused by his animosity toward the captain. He had just come in quietly. He seemed reserved and thoughtful.

"You've examined those ships?"

"Yes," replied the xenologist. "I know their general lines, their means of propulsion, but less than an hour's study is not enough to . . ."

"It's your impressions we want."

The stars and the moving dots disappeared from the screens. An enormous alien ship appeared in their place, enlarged so greatly that the details were blurred. But its spindle shape was clear. All sorts of appendages, masts, propellers, perhaps armaments stuck out from what was the hull.

"That ship was built by humans, or at least humanoids," commented Smirno.

"Is that an opinion or a certitude?"

"A near certitude. There are close ties between the technology of an intelligent species and its physical aspect. All the characteristics of an object are conceived in relation to its user. I think we should have no difficulty in manning one of those ships were we to capture it."

"That ship is less than five light-years away," Shangrin interrupted. "Five light-years ago it was cruising in these parts. Since then, it probably reached its destination. But the civilization that produced it is still extant. It's waiting for us."

He pointed to the ghost ship on the screen.

"Zoltan maintains that no humans can sustain life in this era. He is probably right. Smirno says that this ship was probably built by men. We know how competent he is. At first glance, their opinions seem incompatible."

Shangrin smiled broadly. He was skillfully setting the stage.

"But there remains our voyage in time. Zoltan and Smirno could both be right. If the men in command of those ships come from the past, they control time."

"Do you want to make contact with them?" Nardi asked.

"Certainly. As soon as we detected those ships, I stopped everything. We have given up intergalactic operations in favor of interstellar speed. In a few minutes we'll reintegrate into normal space. We are headed for the system from which those ships seem to have come. It consists of six planets, two of which appear to be habitable. If those people have the secret of voyaging in time, well, we'll squeeze it out of them. If they are the ones responsible for dragging us from the future, we'll make them regret it. If they want to be friends, we'll trade with them. If they want to be enemies, we'll wage war."

"Shangrin," said Nardi, "you're awfully sure of yourself. You know things that no one else knows and now you are proposing to defeat people who have a power we don't possess and which represents a fantastic knowledge of physics. You haven't answered my accusation."

"There's nothing to be said against a monstrous absurdity," bellowed Shangrin. "You're more experienced than I am, Mr. Nardi, but I have one skill you do not possess: I am a chess player. Because of this I can recognize a superior intelligence when I meet one. It has given me, even here, an invaluable ally. I won't keep from you any longer that it is to him that I owe the few bits of information which have suprised you so much."

Something came in. The council had some difficulty at first in recognizing what it was. It looked like a metallic contraption holding up something that moved. It looked like a huge orange crab set on a gigantic ball of wool. A woman screamed. Several men got up, threateningly.

"Quiet," Shangrin shouted. "This is my ally. The Runi. I didn't know, when I surreptitiously brought him on board, how useful he would turn out to be. I ask you to give him a warmer welcome. He's our only hope for getting back to our time."

He was too strange to be frightening, Norma thought. A chess-playing monster. No, there's really nothing human about him. . . . How could he help us? Except that he's alone. He, too, is lost in the past and wants to get back to his own world. Without us, he hasn't the slimmest chance of getting there. She saw Smirno get up, but she paid little atention to what he was saying.

"In the present circumstances, we could censure Captain Shangrin as easily as we could reaffirm our faith in him. He has broken the law in every conceivable way. But it could well be that his very lack of respect for the law is now our salvation. Whatever my feelings toward him, I suggest that in the interest of the ship we reinstate the mandate of the captain and of his first mate."

"I object!" shouted Nardi.

But his voice was drowned out in the general uproar. The robot-ushers emitted a strident whistle that was agony to the ears. Silence was restored.

"Have you anything more to add, Captain?" asked an usher.

"Just this," Shangrin replied calmly, almost solemnly. "A piece of advice to my young and explosive opponents: the best way to win a war is to cooperate with the enemy, to win his help. That's all."

The voting procedure was brief. Eighty-seven percent of the council members confirmed Varun Shangrin's mandate and trusted him to deal with the crisis. Varun Shangrin, once more, had got his own way.

CHAPTER V

The most surprising thing was the normal, almost familiar aspect of the alien ship. An abyss of time separated its builders from the Magellanites, but the latters' ancestors had piloted ships similar to that one in the Prime-Galaxy. And according to legend, they had crossed the intergalactic gap on ships scarcely more powerful during the course of an incredibly long voyage.

Shangrin, ensconced in his large chair, was carefully filling his teapot. Smirno nervously looked at the navigation charts. Gregory dictated orders to a robot.

"Eighty-seven ships in action in the system of stars we have just entered."

"That's not very many," said Shangrin.

"It's obviously a civilization still in the cradle," answered Smirno. He was plainly trying to cooperate, to conceal his hatred for the captain as well as he could. "It's just beginning interstellar travel. I very much doubt that you will discover any way of crossing the time barrier here."

The stellar system was made up of seven stars relatively close to one another. There were less than twelve light-years between the most distant of them; the closest ones were separated by less than one light-year. All of these stars were surrounded by planets that were habitable at various stages of their evolution. These conditions were ideal for a quick discovery of the route to space. This civilization must have gradually progressed from interplanetary voyages to interstellar expeditions. If tradition was to be believed, there had been no need for a technological revolution such as humanity had required.

"I don't think they know how to travel in time," agreed Shangrin. "I do think that they were brought there and that they can probably lead us back to whoever's pulling the strings."

"Do you think they're our contemporaries or do they come from our future? And why should they know more than we do? They could have been projected here, just as we were."

Gregory stopped dictating.

"It could be possible that we are in some sort of trap, an immense oubliette in time. That's it. Just imagine a civilization in the distant future setting traps all over space and time. All those who fall into them rush headlong into the past. If their technology is sufficiently advanced, they survive. They regress for awhile, then leave. They start the whole process of colonizing the planets around them all over again."

He indicated the mobile dots on the screen.

"They may very well not know where they come from. As for us, it was a close call. Without the Runi, we would never even have known that we'd moved in time, not space."

Shangrin objected.

"Not right away, but we would have known. Derin, the metrologist, was on the right path. The mass of the universe—of each object—was changed. We would have discovered it."

"Yes, but these people might not have. On the other hand, a powerful people is not necessarily going to wipe out whatever falls into one of its traps. Just imagine a gigantic war between several galaxies. A myriad ships tumble into the moats that protect the fortresses of the stars. Who gives a thought to the frogs and mosquitoes in the castle moats?"

"Maybe," Shangrin conceded. "But I'm more inclined to believe that the masters of time keep an eye on what is teeming in their dungeons, that they come and fish in their moats every so often. I'll climb back up again, if it is humanly possible. I'll buy back our freedom."

"Providing you have something they want," the xenologist interrupted.

"I didn't have anything to sell the Runi either."

The xenologist made a face. He didn't like to be reminded of the Runi affair—especially when the reminder came from Shangrin. He pretended to examine the alien ship, now less than a quarter of a light-year away. It might not even have reached its destination since this particular image had become detached from it and had traveled in space to reach them.

"The portholes are clearly visible," he said. "That means they have not yet conquered Second Space. Everything works out."

He turned to Shangrin.

"And those broadcasts we heard so much about?"

"They are going to be transmitted, any moment now, as soon as the image is clearer."

The xenologist stared at Shangrin. He was aware of the sarcasm that underlay the captain's every word. You're an expert, Shangrin seemed to imply, and nothing but, and I am making use of you.

The xenologist looked at Gregory, who was poring over charts. He thought that ambition was written all over the first mate. Smirno's own talent lay in uncovering people's passions and their weaknesses, the cracks in their armor, their breaking points. Gregory wanted Shangrin's position, Smirno surmised, and when he had attained it, he would be just like him. More cautious perhaps, even craftier, less overbearing. But, basically, just as despotic. And in Shangrin's Olympian face, the xenologist could detect greed and a taste for power as well. That was the way they were. They were both powerful men, and he did not like them.

And what was his own main interest? He wondered and found no answer. Science? Not even that. He liked living, to be sure. But unlike most Magellanites, he did not believe in happiness. He was bored and growing old. He was tired of being carted about in that old sphere, the *Vasco*. He rather envied the two men because their activity seemed to satisfy them. His prime passion, he recognized, was jealousy.

What is a xenologist? Smirno asked himself. A fifth wheel, a man who went along on intersidereal expeditions and who, nine times out of ten, served no useful purpose. That tenth time, suddenly, he was obliged to shoulder a tremendous responsibility: making contact with another form of life, with another form of intelligence. He knew a little bit about everything, Smirno acknowledged, but possessed no deep knowledge of anything because his field was too broad. He had a mountain of file cards: all the data available, on cards, of alien life, of non-human civilizations. A xenologist was a gentleman who endlessly filed cards. If he was lucky, he contributed a few new ones.

The functions of xenologists in the document rooms of core worlds were entirely different. They reshuffled information and built up theories. Now that, Smirno felt, was passionately interesting and gave a meaning to life. That was more than just making a hodgepodge of linguistics, biology, psychology, physics and intuition— plus a large dose of imagination—for the formulation of some theory about a species of which nothing positive was known.

The standing joke among explorers was; What is xenology? Answer: an art that miscarried, a judgment that was unfortunately justified. A good xenologist ought to sniff out the unusual, be suspicious of abstractions, except on central worlds. There, Smirno thought again, a xenologist could really use his brain. If he ever got back to the Lesser Magellanics, perhaps he would get a research post. But he no longer hoped to return. They would never be able to cross over two hundred million years; he would never come into his own.

He picked his words carefully.

"Listen, Shangrin. I agreed to work with you because of circumstances. But if by any chance we do get back to Neo-Sirius I'll lodge a complaint against you. I'll tell them everything you've done."

"That's great," said Shangrin sarcastically, sniffing the steam escaping from his teapot. "You make just about as much sense as the Runi."

"There they go, they've hooked up the telecast," Gregory exclaimed.

Smirno welcomed the diversion. He was powerless against Shangrin and the captain, on the other hand, would never stop reminding him about the Runis. He simply would not let go.

To the right of the alien ship on the screen they could see a blurred image crackling with flashes of lightning. It grew steadier, shimmering every now and then. A man wearing a strange uniform was speaking heatedly. He had a short black beard that outlined thin, cruel lips. His clothes seemed to be woven of metal thread. Oddly enough, a dagger in a scarlet sheath hung from his belt.

"Barbarians," said Gregory.

"No preconceived notions," interrupted the xenologist.

"Can you understand what he's saying?"

Smirno shook his head.

"I'm not a linguist, but I think I recognize some of the roots. The sound of this language is not very different from ours. It could be a parallel form, or a more developed one."

"The semantics experts are studying the problem," Shangrin said. "I think they'll be able to start translating in a couple of hours. I just wanted your opinion."

Smirno turned angrily.

"You're trying to make me look like a fool."

"Not at all. I have a higher opinion of your capabilities than you have. You don't like me; that's your privilege. It makes things easier for me, but it's unimportant. I need your expertise. We are going to make contact with those people—tomorrow."

"You're going to board one of their ships?"

"No," replied Shangrin, staring at the golden tea in

his cup. "No, I'm going to land on one of their worlds. And possibly conquer it."

Basically, thought Smirno, he hated the captain because of his own mistake with the Runis. But knowing that did not soothe him. It did not do away with his hatred for Shangrin and his smugness any more than knowing the causes of a wound did away with the pain.

The *Vasco* dropped from the skies onto the surface of the planet. It circled several times, like a fiery star, before heading toward its objective, a vast plain near the equator. On the screens, space changed color from black to a lighter and lighter blue. The stars were extinguished, then lighted up again, then disappeared once more while the ship, in a spiraling movement, traversed day and night.

Then came the familiar excitement of seeing a new planet with its continents shrouded in clouds, its high mountains covered with white lace, oceans sparkling in the sun like sheets of metal, inky black at night. There were lights of cities here and there on continents otherwise plunged in darkness. Air traffic was not very heavy and the *Vasco* paid little attention to it. Henrik, Shangrin and Gregory kept a close eye on the spherical navigation screen. It looked like a giant map unrolling evenly.

"You're taking a stupid risk," Henrik said. "Why didn't you put the ship into orbit and send out a reconnaissance boat? You haven't the slightest idea about their defenses."

"I want to impress them," said Shangrin. "And anyway, I do know about their weapons. They are nothing to worry about."

"Besides which, they apparently protect only their cities," observed Gregory.

"Then why have they refused to communicate with us? We've been signaling them on their own frequencies, and they've been sending rockets." Henrik was obviously nervous.

"They are at war . . . they thought it was a trap.

Smirno is studying the photos we've taken of their cities and their plains. Has he made anything of them?"

"He's trying to get some idea of their social structure. But tell me, Shangrin, I thought he disliked you so much because of the Runi affair. How come he's helping you as though nothing had happened?"

"He hates me, all right," said Shangrin. "I know that, but it doesn't matter. He's a cool customer. He won't try anything against me in our present situation. He'll wait until we've gotten out of it."

"If I were you, I wouldn't trust him."

"Why? He's doing his job, that's all. He's the best xenologist on board, and one of the best in Lorne. He has a team of experts that I need, so I trust him. I've noticed that the people who hate me serve me better than those who admire me."

"Xandra, that planet's name is Xandra," said Gregory.

He didn't like the way the conversation was headed, but nothing ever kept Shangrin from finishing his thought.

"You don't like me either, Henrik, you'd like to be in my shoes. At your age I had already been in command of a ship for eight years. You must dream about it. You can see yourself master of the *Vasco*, directing this metal ball between those stars you know so well."

"Come on, Varun. I've never . . ."

"I know. But you'll never be captain, Henrik. You're not ruthless enough. I am ten years older than you and I have twice your energy. I know how to roar, you don't. My mind is subtle; yours is only tortuous."

Henrik's bald pate became purple, a symptom of his fury. Shangrin liked to bait the officers under his command. When he could no longer rouse their anger, when they became indifferent, that would be the end for him. He would lose his hold over men and, consequently, over things. Then he would die.

Smirno's eyes, red-rimmed with fatigue, turned to the screen for the twentieth time. The image was poor and the light too glaring, but if he turned it down, details would be blurred and details were what he was feverishly studying. They would provide a clue to the level of civilization of this people, of their technology, skills, perhaps even their way of thinking.

The screen showed a city, one of the planet's hundred or so, which was not really very many for a civilization that was beginning to deploy itself into space. The buildings, barely visible on the screen, were crowded together inside tall white walls surmounted by massive towers. The cities were, in fact, fortresses.

This was rather peculiar, Smirno thought. The walls could in no way serve as a protection against aerial attack, yet the inhabitants of the cities were obviously afraid of this possibility since they had launched primitive rockets with nuclear heads. The missiles had exploded in the upper atmosphere long before reaching the *Vasco,* unleashing huge fireworks.

Smirno had seen the rockets climbing toward the screen like a bundle of fine glittering needles at the top of a column of smoke. An invisible finger stretched out from the *Vasco* and dispersed them. They exploded in sudden inferno. The temperature reached one million degrees; the light was equal to one sun's. But there was nothing to destroy in the mesosphere of Xandra.

The cities had not sent out a second salvo. They must have realized they could not do anything to the spherical ship falling from the sky.

Plains and mountains were filing past on the screen. Smirno was surprised that the cities were still so crowded within their walls at this stage of civilization. He would have expected the people to have cultivated the surrounding land, built roads, established systems of communication. But that wasn't the case: these cities looked like small autonomous islands, heavily equipped for defense against the plains and jealously guarding their independence. Was there a war going on below? Were armies being deployed in the plains, occupying fortifications, harassing the cities?

It was up to him to discover all this, and he was

sure of almost no single fact. If there were indeed armies down there, they used no advanced method of communication; they had no truly modern weapons; they were not composed of units sufficiently large to be visible on the march or in combat. Could the war be taking place beyond the limits of the planet? Of the whole system? Perhaps the cities were only advance posts of an army determined to conquer Xandra. The ships Smirno had seen on the screens as luminous dots could easily have been in the midst of a battle. The *Vasco* had paid no more attention to their movements than an eagle does to a swarm of flies. An empire might be in the process of being created or undone; the most frightful anarchy could be reigning on Xandra and in all surrounding space and Smirno know nothing about it. He was in the position of a man studying the activity of an ant hill. He understood nothing.

Decoded messages piled up on his desk, but they were not enlightening. The meaning of most of them was too limited to be of interest to him—they referred to people and events he knew nothing about. There was some question of empire, however, or something of the sort, and without exactly knowing why, Smirno had a feeling, from reading the messages, that it was threatened.

The ship stopped twenty meters from the ground in hissing steam, shrieking wind and a howling storm. It floated like a perfect sphere, a polished mountain more than a kilometer high. It was beautiful and strange. No one had ever seen anything like it on Xandra. It was a miracle.

Shangrin burst out laughing.

"We're there. We're going to get a closer look at whoever wanted to tickle us with their atoms."

Smirno droned on: "It looks as if a state of war, at least a latent one, exists between the inhabitants of the plains and those of the cities. I'm not a historian, but the unusually massive fortifications of the cities tend to indicate that their technological superiority does not guarantee them control of the planet. This theory needs—"

"Easy does it," Gregory ordered. "Put down the gliders of groups seven and nine. Not so fast. Easy. Don't break anything. Give them room. How many times must I tell you not to break the field all at once?"

"Radar shows a cavalry group in operation, north-northeast, less than a hundred kilometers away. It seems to be headed in this direction."

"I'm not a biologist," Smirno continued, "but from the looks of the flora and fauna, we can deduce that a truly agricultural society has been in existence on this world only since—"

"Everyone on alert, Plan C. No one is to leave the ship under any pretext whatsoever except the crews who have their orders. Open fire only in defense. Gliders will be armed as usual."

"Courage, my boys," shouted Shangrin. "Gold, loot, trade. You won't be sorry you came."

The *Vasco* was like a hive. Every member of the crew was at his post. Navigators scanned the sky. Biologists and geophysicists were trying to determine in what way Xandra differed from a type-T world. Message Control intercepted wires which cryptanalysts decoded. The men of the defense groups were getting armed.

Shangrin put on his blue dress uniform. His beard, against the dark background of his outfit, gleamed almost as brightly as the large medallion hanging from a chain on his chest. His head and hands were un-covered: he hated protective devices that shielded him from reality, suppressed smells, gusts of wind and the heat of the sun.

The great hatches on the *Vasco's* underbelly opened up and the gliders were let down on the ground. Each of the vast oblong skiffs flew a flag with the Lesser Magellanic coat of arms. The captain's flew his colors, crimson and black.

He filed past the men in formation. Although this was a frequent occurrence, the Magellanites always celebrated their arrival on a new planet with a certain pomp. They saluted him with hurrahs. He had lost none of his popularity with them—he probably never would. Some day, though, he would leave their world and take his place among their legends.

CHAPTER VI

Lo Alabulo saw the first gliders. He was on scout duty, riding his hexapod unicorn, a bow in his right hand, a vronn resting on the leather pad on his left shoulder. The chitinous wings of the vronn vibrated against his bearded cheek, making the air resound with a shrill death chant.

He closed his eyes halfway in order to see more clearly the shadows which raced over the plain at incredible speeds. They floated in the air. They flew like vronns, although they had no wings—and they were flying straight at him. There were seven of them.

Lo Alabulo pulled in the reins suddenly. His mount reared, turned about as he spurred him on, bolted away. The vronn, on Lo Alabulo's shoulder, unfurled his wings and steadied himself against the wind of their course.

"Foreigners," Lo shouted to the Sar. The Sar raised his lance in combat position. The foreigners had arrived in that ball of fire from the sky. The Sar looked upon everything that came from the sky as being inimical except, of course, the ships that mysteriously seemed to obey the Ulsar. They brought arms to fight against the cities. But those ships were as pointed as arrows and they gave out signals in the sky before landing. These foreigners had made no such signals. They were probably allies of the city dwellers and were, no doubt, coming to their rescue. But the fearsome weapons lent to the Ulsar by his allies would take care of them. The Sar was sure of it. He had already destroyed several of the cities' great ships which had either accidentally fallen on his land or which had, with foolhardy temerity, come to challenge him.

The speed of the approaching vessels worried the Sar. The hexapods' strength lay in their mobility but, compared to these skiffs, their speed was tortoise-like. The aircraft seemed to be animated by a frightful wind which made the grass bow down.

The Sar gave the order to attack. His horsemen dispersed and Lo Alabulo resumed his scouting post. The vronn, sharing his master's excitement, made his wings vibrate harder. The Sar, in his chariot, smiled as he fingered sun grenades capable of melting rock and annihilating any enemy.

The gliders stopped three arrow-lengths from Lo. He had expected them to dive-bomb him so he had drawn his bow, keeping the arrow in his teeth, ready to release the vronn. When he saw the men in the skiffs, he shouted insults at them. He made his hexapod rear and pivot to show them he was not afraid, that he was ready to sacrifice his life. The gods had ordered the destruction of the demons who ruled the cities; this was the price the plains people had to pay for their freedom.

He released the vronn. The insect shot out like an arrow, catapulted by Lo's powerful wrist. It climbed high and circled twice. Then, having selected its prey, a red giant in the front of the biggest skiff, it dived down, wings immobile, legs folded under, fang ready to dart its poison.

The vronn's sting was fatal. It injected almost a quarter of a liter of a poison so strong that the game it killed was inedible. Vronns were used exclusively in warfare.

The vronn stopped suddenly in mid-flight and plummeted to the ground. Someone from the skiff had killed it with an invisible weapon.

Lo was overcome with anger and grief. The vronn had been as a brother. It had saved his life in many a battle. Lo Alabulo gave a bloodcurdling shout and spurred his mount to a gallop, releasing an arrow as

he rode. He had the satisfaction of seeing a man in one
of the skiffs collapse. He turned around and saw the
Sar following with his men. A volley of arrows sailed
over his head as he reloaded his bow.

A volley of fire hit him full in the chest, raised him
from his mount and threw him on the ground. He heard
the hexapod scream and saw it writhe in the flames.
Then pain was joined to anger and grief and Lo Alabulo,
his bow broken, rested with his gods.

"Barbarians," said Smirno. "They are going to attack."

"Not yet," answered Shangrin. "I know how to deal
with them. Don't move."

The barbarian closest to them was executing a senseless maneuver with his mount. Suddenly he stretched
out his arm and something flew off his shoulder. They
could not quite make out what it was.

"A rocket, some mechanical contraption?"

They let the thing come closer.

"An insect," said Gregory. "A giant insect."

Smirno agreed.

"They must train them for hunting. I've seen men on
other planets use birds in the same way. I'm sure that
a stinger that size can kill a man."

Gregory pulled out his weapon and shot. The giant
insect was felled, hitting the ground with a dull thud.

Almost immediately they heard a hissing sound. They
ducked instinctively. Behind them, one of the men cried
out and fell.

"An arrow," someone said.

"He's dead."

"Look out," yelled Gregory.

Defense fields were instantly drawn and tidily blocked
off the volley of arrows. Only the first ones had penetrated to the gliders, wounding and killing a few men.

The Sar, from the top of his chariot, saw with aston-
ishment the arrows of his warriors flattened against an
invisible barrier. He did not believe in the gods, but he

knew that men from space had strange powers. He smiled. Everything gave way before the sun grenades. He singled one out, patted it, pulled the pin, then hurled it.

Gregory tried to guess the intentions of the motionless horsemen. Only the archer had been shot and brought down before Shangrin gave the order not to retaliate.

Night was drawing near. On the horizon, the endless stretch of grass was becoming lavender-tinted. The soil was spongy, which explained the scarcity of trees.

"They surely don't know how to travel in time," Gregory said.

Shangrin turned toward him.

"You think so? They look straight out of the past."

"It's going to be difficult to approach them now that there have been casualties."

"I know," Shangrin answered curtly. "What are our losses?"

"Four dead, seven wounded."

"They were brave men," Shangrin said.

"If we had taken more precautions, they would still be."

Shangrin shot him a surprised look.

"You don't trust me anymore?"

"That's not it; only those deaths were unnecessary."

"One can never take all possible precautions. Whoever tries to protect himself all the time gets nowhere. Was I less exposed than those men?"

"No," admitted Gregory.

He saw a shining sphere rise above a war chariot drawn by two animals that certainly seemed to have six legs. It did not hesitate the way the insect had, but aimed straight for its goal.

"Screen," said Shangrin. "An atomic grenade."

He was not sure the protective screen would hold so he pushed aside a gunner and grabbed the controls of a heavy weapon. The cannon spat out a tongue of fire to meet the grenade. Other shots framed it.

It exploded. The sky became white, the color of over-heated metal. The protection field attenuated the wave of the shock and deflected it back toward the barbarians.

The Sar was hurled from his chariot. The shock had thrown the animals and perhaps killed them. The chariot had lost its wheels. It was a miracle that he himself had not been killed.

He got up painfully, drew his small sword and looked about him. Some of his men were fleeing toward the north. Some of them were trying to keep their mounts from running away with them. Others had broken a limb or so in their fall and were groaning.

It was a disaster. The grenade had exploded much too soon. Usually it didn't explode until it had hit its objective, but the invaders' fingers of fire had touched it and its mysterious mechanism had gone off.

The Sar blamed himself for having allowed Lo Alabulo to act. He could perhaps have made an alliance with the foreigners and thus brought credit on himself with his clan. He might even have lowered the credit of the Ulsar, who had become insufferable since his allies from other worlds had taken him into space—he now claimed that the gods had spoken to him.

And now the fingers of fire were going to touch him, the Sar. The gliders approached slowly, floating in the air like boats upon water. The Sar raised his sword to fight. The skiffs could run him over, but he would die with his sword in his hand.

A huge voice burst over him. It spoke the language of the cities, a language quite similar to that of the plains people except for a different accent. Long ago that shade of difference had indicated caste and it could still anger the Ulsar.

But the voice spoke of peace. It praised the courage of the plains people and asked for an alliance with them; it promised riches.

Surprised, the Sar stopped. Then he looked at his sword and he began to laugh.

Shangrin's voice thundered and rolled in the wind with the majesty of the sea. It swelled and climbed skyward, then became soft and persuasive and slipped through the grasses. It said glorious, imperious, threatening, friendly things.

"We are merchants," Shangrin said. "There are many worlds in the sky and we go from one to another, and everywhere, always, we bring happiness and wealth. We come from powerful worlds and we control powerful forces, but we are peaceful men. We do not want to take either your possessions or your lives."

The Sar hesitated. This could be a pack of lies, but these men could already have struck him down if they had wanted to. He was wearing amulets, but he did not believe in their efficacy. Lo Alabulo had also worn some and he was now dead. The Ulsar did not wear any and he was feared and respected. In any event, the Sar was now at their mercy.

He threw down his sword and walked on the grass toward the skiffs. Then the largest of them landed and a door opened, like an eye in its side. A large man with a red beard came down four metal steps.

He too walked in the grass toward the Sar and put out his hand.

The Sar couldn't believe his eyes. Surely that enormous sphere come down from the sky was a star, but it was cold to the touch. He had looked for a long time at the stream of men pouring out of it, then being swallowed up again, before making up his mind to set foot inside. The red-bearded man urged him on. In the the end, he had given in. He wanted to know what the inside of a star was like.

And he had seen gold, weapons, grenades more powerful than those of the pirates. He had seen the men from the star look after their wounded companions and bring some back to life—even those he would have ordered finished off.

He had been questioned.

He had distrusted them. Why did they want to know

if his group was alone, the location of his camp, who
was the Ulsar, with whom they were at war, if other
men regularly came from space?

He had been plied with gold. A stronger sword than
the one he had left in the grass had been hung by his
side. He had been given a pistol like the ones the men
from the star carried, an odd sort of weapon which induced sleep rather than death.

He had burst out laughing and during the banquet he
had answered all their questions.

No, he was not alone. His group was part of a large
army under the command of the Ulsar. The Sar was
one of his lieutenants. He thought the Ulsar was the
commander-in-chief of the planet. Yes, he was a hard,
pitiless man, but he was fair. He was trying to wipe
the cities off the face of the planet. It was a necessary
war. Once upon a time, the cities had enslaved the
plains people.

Long ago?

The Sar dug back in his memory. It was before he
was born. There were stories old warriors knew, and
the Ulsar had told them to his troops to urge them on.
In olden times, the Sar wasn't sure when, people had
been happy on Xandra. They had cities and cultivated
the land, but hunting was their chief occupation.

Then men had come down from the sky, another
breed. They were not numerous, but nothing could
stand against their weapons. They had forced the inhabitants of Xandra to build cities for them and serve
them.

This had gone on for a long time. Rebellions had
broken out but they had always been suppressed. As
the years went by, though, the people in the cities had
become careless. They took in slaves and sometimes
even raised them to their level.

Weapons had been stolen. A new rebellion had broken
out and almost succeeded. The army of the first Ulsar
captured three cities and razed them to the ground. The
Ulsar was exceedingly able: it was said that the gods
had helped him. He had spared some interplanetary

spaceships and had forced their former captains to pilot them for him, venturing out toward the stars. He had never returned from his last trip, but it was said that some of his ships had become pirates and merchants. It was these ships which supplied arms to the present Ulsar, who had entered into strange and terrible alliances in the sun country. The Ulsar even said that in other worlds there was the same sort of struggle as on Xandra, and that some day soon all the former slaves would unite and hunt down their oppressors to the ends of the universe.

"What do you think about all this, Smirno?" asked Shangrin.

The xenologist was looking at a screen on which bright lights shone, some steadily, some intermittently: city and airplane lights.

"We'll have to meet that Ulsar," he said. "The Sar is only a warrior. The other seems to be a man of stature, a statesman."

Shangrin nodded.

"I'm going to see the Ulsar; I'm going to propose an alliance."

"I doubt if he knows anything about our problem. The arms suppliers might, but it's a long way from interplanetary navigation and nuclear grenades to travel in time. Why not get in touch with the city people instead?"

Shangrin made a face.

"They know less than the Ulsar. They are losing momentum and, besides, I don't like them. Have you seen the snapshots that the scouts brought back?"

"No," said Smirno.

Silently, Gregory handed them to the xenologist.

They had been taken with a powerful telephoto lens. They showed part of a thick wall. At the foot of the wall there were pyramids of human skulls.

Smirno shuddered.

"Genghis Khan," he said. "Hitler. Tarn."

"I don't know those names," said Shangrin, "but I can tell a genocide when I see one."

"They're barbarians," said Gregory.

Smirno shook his head.

"No, they're not barbarians. They're worse—they're civilized. They erect those pyramids for the same reason we dress up a scarecrow. They either despise or hate inanely their former slaves. Or both."

"Do you want to know what I think?" asked Gregory. "Xandra was settled in population waves. A long time ago, perhaps several thousand years, a giant spaceship, or a fleet of spaceships, landed on this world, possibly after having crossed the time barrier the way we've done. The passengers survived, settled down and started off almost from scratch. Almost. You've noticed that the Sar had a certain familiarity with astronomy and that he knows something about nuclear explosives."

."His people may have learned those things in the cities."

"Maybe, but I don't think so. I think, rather, that they form part of the oral tradition of the plains people and that they are now becoming useful once more. But to come back to my theory: a long time after this first catastrophe, a second wave of immigrants settled on this world. They, too, must have come from the future, probably accidentally and with no hope of return—they would not indulge in an uncertain war otherwise. But they preserved their technology. And they found, in the very presence of the first wave of settlers, the means of preserving it: slave labor to build cities and forge arms. All they needed to do was help themselves. Then they took on the mentality of their slaves and decadence set in."

Shangrin put his hands on Gregory's shoulders.

"Good for you. Someday, if you'll drink tea, you'll be as clever as I am. But you missed the most important point."

"What's that?"

"We are the third wave."

Stunned, Gregory looked at Smirno, then back again at Shangrin. He noticed that over his usual clothes,

Shangrin was wearing a tunic woven of fine red metal. What an odd idea, he thought.

"What are you going to do now?" asked Smirno.

"I've told you. Enter into an alliance with the Ulsar and take all the cities one by one. Conquer the entire planet."

"And then what? That won't give us the key to time."

"Then there's space. You've left out a second point in your analysis, Gregory."

"The other worlds," said Smirno.

"Precisely. There are two empires at war, Gregory. One is rising from its ashes and shaking off the yoke of the second one which had destroyed it. But within the memory of the one or the other, behind the one or the other, there surely lies the secret we are after. We'll buy it, or we'll snatch it."

"Two empires," said Gregory.

"No, at least three," Shangrin corrected. "Two empires plus the Magellanites."

CHAPTER VII

He took a deep breath, but the air of the imitation park did not have that odor of earth and water, of wind and night which pervaded the atmosphere of Xandra. The prospective was also all wrong: the sky was too low; there was no depth. Before, during the long trip, Gregory used to come into the imitation park to try to establish contact with nature, to get a feeling of space. After coming out of a narrow stateroom and a rectilinear corridor, the imitation park had given him the feeling of open space.

He saw Norma among the children. She liked looking after them. After they had returned to Lorne, perhaps he would marry her, but he hadn't the courage to mention it until the crisis was over. He thought about the children. What would happen to them if the *Vasco* did not manage to get back across those two ,hundred million years? How many generations would it take before they reverted to a barbaric state?

She caught sight of him and ran toward him. He took her in his arms and kissed her.

"Not in front of the children," she said.

He began to laugh.

"When can we go out, Gregory? I'll be so glad to be in the open air again. I'd like them to know what a real planet is."

"Not now. The planet is unsafe. Its inhabitants are barbarians."

"So I heard. But are you going?"

"I don't have any choice. Anyway, they're not very dangerous."

"What is he going to do?"

66

"The captain? He wants war."

She shot him a horrified look.

"He wants to attack the cities—he thinks he'll find the beginning of a solution there. The inhabitants refuse to communicate with us."

She pulled away, looking at the children.

"He put on quite a performance at the council meeting," she said, "but he frightens me. I don't like his laugh. And why did he drag in that monster?"

"The Runi? I helped bring him on board the *Vasco*!"

"Why?"

"Because Shangrin wanted it. And you just don't argue when he gives an order."

"But it was illegal."

"Not for him. And the Runi could have meant a huge profit."

"Gregory! How can you balance a profit, no matter how sizable, against the safety of the entire ship?"

"The Runi is no threat to the ship," he said. "On the contrary, he's our only hope of salvation."

She did not pursue the point, but looked at him with her light eyes, appearing surprisingly young and determined. He knew she was not very intelligent, but that was not what he was looking for.

"And this war?" she asked. "Has he any right to carry it on?"

"That doesn't matter. The right to do so won't come into existence for two hundred million years."

"It will for me. Are you going to go along?"

"I think so. There's no alternative, and he's a brilliant commander."

"I'm going to try to stop you, Gregory, if you go too far. All this means more casualties, more suffering."

He was unable to repress a smile. The girl's indignation was that of all the women of the Lesser Magellanics: they were self-assured, the representatives of time, security and the law; they acted as surer brakes to the daring of their men than an army of judges. Nonetheless, they brought out the best in the men, as they intuitively fought for their children, for the future of the race, against blind greed.

Shangrin and Norma . . . the struggle seemed too uneven, but it wasn't. Maybe someday some woman might be able to sway the old loner who had triumphed over space and alien races, avoided the ambushes of new worlds and made questionable deals—and who had now taken on time itself.

It took them four days to reach the Ulsar's camp. The gliders could have gone across the grassy plains and reached the foothills of the mountains in a few hours, but Shangrin preferred to go at the slow pace of his allies' mounts. He felt it would be a poor idea to show off his power. Furthermore, he was flattering the Sar.

The horsemen were in front. Shangrin and the Sar rode in the middle. The captain was mounted on the beast of a dead warrior; he wore his red metal tunic and carried a fine steel sword, looking as though he had at last found his place in the scheme of things. One might have guessed that he had spent his life traveling over the great plains, sword in hand, red beard flying in the wind. The Sar had abandoned his wrecked chariot and refused Shangrin's offer to have a new one built for him. He had, however, accepted the tungsten sword which the foreigners had forged for him in atomic fire.

The gliders followed, carrying Shangrin's men, Gregory, Smirno and two combat groups. It was a delegation of thirty men. They all wore mail tunics and swords, but they had more deadly weapons in their pockets. Shangrin trusted no one absolutely.

They rode for four days without Shangrin's showing any signs of fatigue. The Sar was impressed that the use of machinery had in no way impaired the strength of these foreigners as it had that of the city dwellers. For hours on end, the Sar talked with Shangrin and he conceived tremendous respect for the powerful civilization which had produced such a man. He told himself that he had finally met a man whose personality was stronger than the Ulsar's. Had Shangrin asked him to follow him into space, he would unhesitatingly have done so.

They went northward on a complicated itinerary through a marshy labyrinth. For one whole day, the animals were chest-high in water; floating grass got caught on the riders' spurs, creating a green wake. Then the ground hardened and they crossed narrow gaps dug by violent winds thousands of years earlier, when great glaciers had overrun the plateau. Around noon of the fourth day, they reached the rocky hills. It was hot and dry, and the blue thickets were teeming with game. They made a wide detour in under to avoid a nest of wild vronns. They spotted it because the hill was too symmetrical; one could guess, despite the distance, that it consisted of chambers, corridors, wells. It was a spongy mixture of rocks, soil and sand piled up by the saliva of the killers in chitinous armor.

The thin smoke of fires in the Ulsar's camp made stripes in an evening sky whose smooth purity was like fine silk or polished metal. Banners bearing the Ulsar's monogram floated at the top of tall poles. A lookout struck a gong and blew into a huge bullhorn. All at once, everything went into motion. The weapons of the warriors glistened above the camouflage. The Sar gave an arm signal and, in response, a standard in his colors was hoisted up a pole. Double wooden doors opened and a cloud of children ran toward the newcomers.

Shangrin signaled to the glider pilots to cut their engines. Studying the Ulsar's city through field glasses, Gregory saw palisades covered with vegetation, concealing interior arrangements. The flags lent a military aspect to the place, but the city still looked more like a temporary camp than a settlement. The Ulsar's supporters must be semi-nomads. There had once existed warlike civilizations of that sort in the dim recesses of the history of humanity. By and large, they had left unpleasant memories behind.

Gregory said to himself that perhaps this was the result of prejudice. History had always been engraved on stone or written on paper by city people who had no sympathy for nomads. From an objective point of view, cities were surely no more civilized nor less cruel, even if their technology was superior. In this world, however, they did seem to be more savage, which probably stemmed from the numerical inferiority of their inhabitants.

Shangrin, riding abreast the Sar, went into the camp. He saw a sort of crater, with perfectly aligned tents filling the bottom. The limits of the camp were marked off by other tents and wooden structures. It must have been huge, for a corral near the crater walls seemed to hold myriad hexapods. Beyond it, the crater looked even deeper. Perhaps there were deep caves or gullies.

A man dressed in especially bright colors was watching their approach from the midst of a small group of warriors. The Sar jumped off his mount and prostrated himself before him. Shangrin decided it must be the Ulsar.

He betrayed none of the disappointment he felt. He had expected a large man, confident of his strength, prepared to challenge him to a fight, verbally or physically, ready to annihilate him with a word or a blow.

The Ulsar was a small, brown man with bright, nervous eyes. He carried no weapons. A cuff from one of the giants around him could have felled him. He must have been outstandingly smart to wield so much authority over a people for whom brute force had lost none of its power. He wasn't even of the same race as the warriors around him. He might be an extraordinary case of atavism, Shangrin considered, or he might have come from a city. Perhaps he had switched sides, leaving behind the race of conquerors. History had often seen liberators recruited from the ranks of the oppressors.

"Greetings," said Shangrin without dismounting.

The Ulsar smiled. It was neither a disquieting nor

disagreeable smile. It was just an intelligent, almost friendly one.

"Welcome," he said.

Two guards helped Shangrin dismount.

"I come from up there," he said, pointing emphatically to the sky.

"From the stars," said the Ulsar.

"Yes," said Shangrin, somewhat taken aback.

He signaled to his two escorts, who jumped down from their hexapods and handed him some boxes.

"Your Sar told me of your power," Shangrin said. "We are merchants. We want to do business in a peaceful way with this land. We want to be your friends."

Shangrin spoke clearly and politely, with no trace of obsequiousness. He opened the boxes.

But the Ulsar did not put out his hand. He said coldly, "Gifts establish friendships between equals. Are you the leader of your people?"

"I am the leader of my people," Shangrin said quickly. "We are many. We live in a ship that has been traveling through space. The Sar has seen it and can describe it."

"I believe you."

Shangrin gave the boxes back to his men. The Ulsar was certainly the first chieftain who did not throw himself on the gifts offered to him: the Ulsar was no barbarian. Shangrin wished that Smirno were there, but the xenologist had remained with Gregory.

"I'll see you tonight," said the Ulsar. "You'll sleep in my tents."

He stopped. His bright black eyes stared deeply into Shangrin's and, it seemed to the Magellanite, somewhat sardonically.

"Why don't you tell those of your men who stayed outside to bring in their machines? They can easily park them in here. Unless they're afraid of hexapods and children."

Shangrin showed signs of irritation.

"The gate is too narrow."

"I've taken a close look at those contraptions," said

the Ulsar, blinking. "I'm sure they can fly over the walls. After all, they went through space, between worlds."

"I think they can," said Shangrin, "but we did not come down from the stars in these. . . ."

"No," said the Ulsar. "No. You came in that large spherical ship."

Shangrin bit his lip. Was the Ulsar telepathic? Was that his hold over his men? If he could read Shangrin's mind that was only the beginning of complications.

"I'll send one of my men with a message," Shangrin capitulated.

"Oh," said the Ulsar, "I think you've forgotten those little gadgets for communication at a distance which men from the stars always carry."

"True," said Shangrin.

He put his hand up to his mouth and whispered a few orders to Gregory. He did not want to give the Ulsar the impression that their entire conversation had been bugged, if the Ulsar did not know it.

"We'll talk some more tonight," said the Ulsar. "The Sar will show you to your tents."

He turned on his heel and left. But after taking a few steps, he stopped and looked over his shoulder.

"You may keep all the arms you want. I trust you. I want you to feel that you are my guests."

Shangrin turned to his men with a helpless look. The shadows cast by the great gliders passed silently by, then the sky cleared and the wind they had made died down. They came down gently in the square outlined by the tents.

This was going to be tough, thought Shangrin. And if it was a trap, they were certainly in it.

The tents were luxuriously appointed. Crystal decanters containing precious liquors were placed on fine tables made of rare wood. The floors were covered with furs; weapons hung from bone stands; leather saddle-shaped chairs formed a circle around an engraved copper hearth.

Shangrin, Gregory and Smirno were thoughtfully warming their hands in front of the fire.

"His manners are those of a barbarian, but he's too knowledgeable," said Smirno.

"He's traveled through space," Gregory reminded them.

"What I'd like to know," said Shangrin, stroking his beard, "is where he really comes from."

There was a teapot warming by the fire. Shangrin was keeping a careful eye on the boiling of the water. He picked up the teapot and threw in a pinch of aromatic herbs.

"I don't believe it's a trap," Gregory said. "He seems to be sizing up our strength pretty accurately. He knows that even if he were to wipe us out, here, he would still have to contend with the ship—which is just about indestructible, at least to him, and capable of destroying the entire planet."

Smirno agreed. "He knows he's vulnerable; that's why he was so haughty. He wants us to know he's not afraid of us. I think that's how he became the Ulsar. I wouldn't put a penny on him in a fight against one of his warriors."

Shangrin was sniffing his tea.

"Who knows? I looked him over closely. He gives every appearance of being frail, but I'll bet he's strong, and only about forty years old. If he knows how to fight, if he has some knowledge of human anatomy and the nervous system, he can kill an opponent twice his size. Barbarians usually don't know how to fight. You have to know what's under the skin to fight properly."

"Where could he have learned?"

"We keep coming back to the same question: Where does he come from? But you're right. He was suspicious and he wanted to show that he was not to be outmaneuvered, that I couldn't count on him for the conquest of the cities."

"He wanted it made clear from the start that he is your equal. The initial impression was that he was doing you a favor, but actually, he was making it plain that he was your equal, that a scruffy leader of a small army of barbarians was as good as a space captain."

"He's hardly a scruffy leader," said Shangrin with an ambiguous smile. "I was expecting a sort of martial lightning bolt, with quick reactions, and I find a crafty diplomat. I wonder how he would do at chess?"

"Why not teach him?" asked Smirno. "It would be an excellent ground for understanding."

"Or for misunderstanding. No, I might be beaten. It's the Runi I'd like to see here. His advice would be valuable—he's a profound thinker."

"About the physical universe, perhaps," said Smirno. "But about humanity . . ."

"He's a chess player. And humans are the pieces on the chessboard of the universe."

"His presence might irritate or even frighten the Ulsar," said Gregory.

"Do you think so?" Shangrin asked sardonically, sipping his tea. "I rather think he is the Runi's blood brother."

The Ulsar's dinner went off in the best barbarian tradition, Smirno thought. It was almost too ostentatious. Serfs had set up tables under a huge tent. The Ulsar's table, to which the three Magellanites were escorted, dominated the banquet hall from a dais. The Ulsar had not yet arrived. His chieftains, in brightly striped, rustling silk tunics, their embossed and jeweled daggers suspended unsheathed from their necks by leather thongs, had sat down in the midst of great noise. They had brought with them heavy pewter tankards, and the serfs—probably captured in raids on the cities—filled them with a light wine.

There was a sudden hush as the Ulsar came in. Slaves, bending under the weight of great coffers, followed him. When he had settled himself in a wooden chair draped with spotted furs, the slaves opened the coffers and set the table with gold plates. On a tripod table at the foot of the dais Shangrin's gifts were displayed: an enormous, finely cut diamond which had lain for a long time in the veins of an asteroid, a set of fine weapons and a mysterious box, set with stones, which Shangrin directed be brought to him. He pushed a spring and the box played sweet music. The Ulsar's barons were filled with wonder, and even he seemed overwhelmed. He filled his goblet, toasted his guest and emptied the remains into a brazier, invoking the gods as he did so.

Was this a trick? wondered Smirno, watching his host clap his hands as course succeeded course. The Ulsar devoured a haunch of venison, grabbing it with both hands. He issued orders and dancing girls appeared. Was all of this nothing but a performance—this vulgar display of barbaric luxury, this excess of everything: colors, sounds, foods, wines, primitive and exciting dances? A girl came and drank from Smirno's cup. He did not doubt her intentions; she was trying to please him. She was beautiful, so he did not repulse her, but he couldn't help wondering if this was all an act. The Ulsar was behaving like a real savage chieftain, talking loudly, clapping his hands, draining cup after cup, laughing and joking with Shangrin, nudging Gregory. Shangrin, splendid in his iridescent tunic, kept up with him. He certainly was playing a part. He was playing it so well that Smirno thought a latent streak of barbarity had been awakened within the captain. Perhaps so. The noisy pleasure he took in the banquet was a natural reaction for him, but nonetheless Smirno knew the captain remained himself, clever, alert.

The Ulsar's liege men were very noisy. Some of them had disappeared under their chairs. Others had climbed up on the tables, their boots clattering against tankards, and were chasing dancers too nimble-footed for their clumsy steps. The Ulsar and Shangrin were talking about hunting. Gregory seemed a trifle withdrawn. Smirno saw him furtively pop a pill into his mouth: a remedy against drunkenness. The captain, although he had drunk as much or more than his host, seemed to be holding his own with no outside help.

Every so often, one of the Sars who was not too drunk would get up from the lower tables and vanish for a few moments. Smirno had a fair idea of his intentions: the human stomach had its limits, whereas during a feast the appetite of a barbarian had none. Then a serf brought the Ulsar a gold basin and the latter stuck two fingers down his throat to vomit. Smirno was unable to stifle a shiver of nausea. He saw with pleasure that Gregory had felt the same revulsion, instantly controlled. Shangrin was superb. He imitated his host's gesture and swept a rapid but angry look at his two cohorts when they declined the slave's services with brief but imperious gestures.

Adjustment. That had ever been the motto of merchants. When in Rome, do as the Romans do. Change your spots. Share. But there were limits, Smirno decided. Supposing the Ulsar was gulling them, pretending, for their benefit, to be a savage chieftain?

The conversation between the Ulsar and Shangrin was taking a different turn. Gregory entered into it every so often, and he almost always sided with the Ulsar. Clever work. Subtle. But the Ulsar was giving nothing away. Shangrin's questions were becoming increasingly direct.

"You're already doing some trading in space?" Shangrin was saying.

The Ulsar smiled slowly.

"We buy arms from dealers. This enables us to fight with more or less equal weaponry against the cities."

"But the cities control space. Deliveries must be rare and irregular."

"I should certainly be happy to buy arms from you," said the Ulsar.

"That would ensure you a quick victory over the cities. You have numbers on your side, haven't you? But the cities remain pretty impregnable."

The Ulsar's face contracted fleetingly.

"That's true."

His speech was slightly thick.

"On the other hand," said Shangrin, "we won't be

able to do much trading with this planet as long as the cities retain control over space."

He leaned toward the Ulsar and whispered: "They launched rockets against us. Obviously, they missed."

"You were prepared to negotiate with them," accused the Ulsar.

Shangrin shook his head.

"We knew nothing about the political situation here. The cities have their own interplanetary routes of trade. They would not have allowed us to compete with them."

He laughed loudly.

"I never meddle in the politics of the worlds with which I trade. It's a principle. But, in a way, I'd like to see you win."

"Oh," said the Ulsar.

He clapped again and a decanter once more hovered over their cups.

"We're brothers, aren't we?" He patted Shangrin's shoulder affectionately.

"Allies," said the captain. "Yes, I think I'd be happy to see you defeat the cities."

"Bullies," said the Ulsar, his head nodding.

"I think I'll give you what you need for victory."

"Cowards."

"Naturally, I expect to have some share in the looting of the cities. And, provisionally, a monopoly on trading with this planet."

"They won't last long now."

"And contact with your suppliers. Perhaps we could put together a fleet and conquer space. I think we could control the whole system. Spread beyond. The cities would retreat everywhere."

"Lots of space pirates," the Ulsar muttered.

"We'll make corsairs out of them," said Shangrin, warming up. "Mercenaries. I can pay them."

Very slowly, the Ulsar straightened out.

"What exactly is it you are looking for?" he asked in a cold, controlled voice that held no trace of drunkenness.

Shangrin pretended to be surprised.

"Oh! Profit," he said in a boozy voice. Smirno kicked him under the table.

"No," said the Ulsar imperiously. "You have something else in mind."

So, it *had* all been an act. He was perfectly sober.

"Power, of course," said Shangrin. "The important thing is to have allies against the cities. It's been a tiring day and a large meal. We'll talk some more to-morrow."

He gestured broadly at the bacchanal unfolding before them. They were almost forced to shout to make themselves heard.

The Ulsar smiled shortly.

"You are no more drunk than I am. Nor are your friends. Waiting is poor counsel, and we're both in a hurry; isn't that right?"

"Yes," Shangrin conceded.

Gregory nodded approval.

The Ulsar stood and clapped, his hands making a brittle sound in the tent. The noise died down and silence ensued. Those in condition to do so turned toward the head table; the dancers stood still. A slave, taken unaware, dropped a goblet that smashed, spilling the wine all over the floor; it made a dark puddle under the torch light.

"Out," said the Ulsar loudly. "Get out, all of you."

CHAPTER VIII

There was a mad rush for the exits. The guests still able to stand staggered out, assisted by the dancers. A horde of slaves rushed toward the others and carried them from the tent. A few came to, protesting, but their voices were drowned out. The girl kneeling at Smirno's feet looked up at him questioningly. He signaled to her to remove herself and she fled.

A second wave of servants cleared the tables by rolling up the tablecloths.

At the head table, the astonished Magellanites looked at the Ulsar. This had been a display of power, to show that he might rule over a gang of barbarians, but he himself was not one. Swallowing a pill to ward off intoxication, Smirno told himself that it all came back to the original question. When they were alone and the Ulsar had sat down again, a look of intense curiosity and also amusement on his face, Smirno was happy to hear Shangrin ask it without beating around the bush.

"Where do you come from? You're not one of them."

"I might ask you the same thing," said the Ulsar. "I've heard about most of the civilizations around us and you don't come from any of them."

Stalemate. Shangrin placed his hands on the table.

"It's enough that we share a common interest in the defeat of the cities. You want to rule this planet and I hope to find certain information there."

"I don't expect to dominate this world," the Ulsar said. "I want to free it from the oppression of the cities."

He added, smiling, "If we are to be allies, we must

be frank with one another. But in order to be frank, we must be allies. It's a vicious circle, isn't it?"

"No," said Gregory. "We can find what we want somewhere else, but you'll never defeat the cities without our help."

"Perhaps," said the Ulsar. "Perhaps you don't need me."

He raised his cup and looked at it, amused.

"Whoever keeps his wine cannot get drunk," he said, then added, "No, I don't come from here. I wasn't even born on this planet. You suspected as much, didn't you?"

Shangrin nodded.

"You see," the Ulsar went on, "the political situation in this region of space is pretty confused. Some years ago a powerful empire stretched out over thirty-odd planets. It particularly bore down on this planet."

"The empire of the cities," said Smirno.

"If you like. We simply call it the Empire. It included a ruling class made up of the descendants of the invaders, and a proletariat, infinitely more numerous, made up of slaves, who were the most ancient people of these worlds. The cruelty of the ruling class was unbelievable. Rebellions broke out here and there but were always ruthlessly repressed. The oppressed peoples of the various planets had no space fleets at their disposal and did not even know, most of the time, of the existence of an intersidereal empire. A revolution, to be successful, must break out simultaneously in several places and the rebels must have a fleet and good communications.

"However, in spite of apparent difficulties, isolated groups in certain worlds did manage to keep going and get properly organized. They even succeeded in infiltrating cities, learning snatches of technology, hijacking ships. There were bitter struggles among them for the ultimate control of the revolutionary movement. One organization survived and won out. When conditions became favorable, it gave the signal for revolt. It sent men to the largest planet of the Empire to foment dissatisfaction and provide leadership in the movement. A war started; it was to be fought in a limited way in space, but, for the most part, on the planets themselves. In the two centuries that this war lasted, the Empire has steadily lost ground. The freedom movement will destroy the oppressors."

The Ulsar's face hardened.

"I belong to this organization—I was sent to Xandra over twenty years ago. My job is almost finished. The ruling class is hanging on only in the cities, in a few decades, Xandra will be free."

"And then what will happen?" Smirno asked.

"I'm not in charge," the Ulsar said curtly. "The battle is now being fought on some sixty-five planets and I am only a cog in the machinery that controls this one. Two or three worlds have already been almost freed. Naturally we have a plan. We want to set up a federation of the planets formerly controlled by the Empire and reawaken in these people, who have returned to a barbaric state, a sense of civilization."

"It's a worthy program," said Shangrin, "but you seem to have rather direct methods."

"We have a war to win. Then we'll see. With your help, we can expedite things."

"What forces in space do you command?"

"Oh, it's simple. The Empire has the better fleet. We ourselves have a few ships through which we deploy agents and distribute arms. And we keep in touch. But the war has given rise to all sorts of other traffic. Some ships that were once owned by our side have more or less turned to pirating. Neighboring federations send out their representatives to distribute arms indiscriminately to the cities or to us. There are easily thirty or forty flagships running into one another in space. The Empire is in the process of collapsing but we are not yet strong enough to take over."

Interregnum, Smirno thought. Looting, anarchy, wars, murder, instability. Bloody battles were being waged in the space through which they had just traveled, confident of their power and speed. Compared to the

supreme power of the Lesser Magellanics, these were
mere skirmishes. But men were dying.

"They don't know that, do they?" asked Gregory.

"My people? Yes. I tell them the truth a little at a
time."

"They think space people are gods."

"That encourages them to face up to the city demons."

Smirno cleared his throat.

"They are not at war for themselves, are they?"

"I'm afraid not," said the Ulsar. "They'll never
know peace. They're fighting for their descendants. And
you—why would you fight?"

"I've already told you," Shangrin began.

"I don't believe you," the Ulsar interrupted violently.
"Skip the rigmarole about profits. It won't stand up.
You're not pirates. You don't belong to any neighboring
civilizations."

"We come from quite a distance," said Gregory.

The Ulsar banged on the table with his fist.

"I'm not asking you where you come from! I'm asking you from what period in time. Time is what concerns
you, isn't it?"

Shangrin whistled through his teeth.

"So you know that too. You know about people
traveling through time."

"Do you think this war would be lasting such a long
time if we could control time? Listen. Neither the con-
querers, the inhabitants, nor any of the surrounding
civilizations originated here. The scientists of the Empire know it although they have lost all trace of the
period when their ancestors were born. But some of our
legends tell of men who went across years as though
they had been rivers. By chance, or perhaps according
to some plan, ships were sent out into space every few
centuries. They came from different periods in time.
You are the most recent and you're trying to get back
to your own period. You are hoping that the cities hold
a key to the mystery. And because they refuse to yield
it up, you want to wrest it from them."

Shangrin made a face.

"And you're not trying to make contact again with the future?"

"What for? We belong here, we have a war to fight. Later, perhaps."

Perfectly logical, Smirno said to himself. They had been born at this period in time; a long chain of generations would have to be gone back over to reach the men who had been thrown into that funnel of time.

But it was a desperate situation. The Empire and its opponents knew or guessed what their own origins were, but they knew nothing about controlling time. Forcing open the gates of the cities would serve no purpose.

The captain got up.

"I'd like to drink a little tea," he said gloomily. "Shall we go into my tent?"

The teakettle was bubbling peacefully. For a fleeting moment, despite the barbaric splendor of his surroundings, Shangrin thought himself back in the control room of the *Vasco*. Then all at once he felt hemmed in by the ghosts of long-ago ships, the remnants of oppressive empires brought to ruin by their own victims. He felt deafened by revolutionary slogans and oppressed by the cold, brutal logic of the tyrant who claimed to be fighting for freedom.

In some respects, the Ulsar seemed to have put himself at Shangrin's mercy. He wondered if this was another subtle trick to influence his decision. He had to take the chance. He might make a wrong move, but even the greatest miscalculation could not make the *Vasco's* case any worse than it was.

In any event, he felt it was better to throw themselves into the battle. If the *Vasco* did not succeed in getting back to its period in time, its passengers would be better off on the winning side. The days of the Empire were numbered. If the *Vasco* helped the rebels win, well then, the Magellanites would be able to play a decisive role in the organization of the future federation, perhaps even a dominant one.

He shook his head.

He knew perfectly well what would happen. The disparity between the technological knowledge of the *Vasco's* crew and that of the rebels was so great that the Magellanites were sure to come out on top. A new form of tyranny would take over in this stellar region, possibly in a more subtle, less crude form than the old one. But a few centuries hence, another revolution would break out. And a second *Vasco* . . .

"And so a great many ships have come from the future," said Gregory, turning toward the Ulsar. "Did some of them have non-human crews?"

The Ulsar had hesitated imperceptibly, Smirno was almost sure. It was difficult to read on a foreign face the emotions of a civilization one hardly knew, but Smirno told himself that this was the first question to catch the Ulsar unprepared. Then he began to doubt, but he never again let his attention wander from the barbarian.

'What do you mean?" said the Ulsar. "I don't see what you're getting at. I don't know of any civilization that is not human."

Was there really a touch of regret in his voice? Smiro wondered. He felt this might provide a hint or a clue to something the Ulsar was hiding. Only a lie detector could tell them for sure.

Shangrin put his hands on his piping-hot teapot.

"Yes," he said. "We've run into some. One of them has become an associate. He has tremendous power; we shall need that, of coure. I'll have to consult him. As a matter of fact, I can't commit myself without asking him."

"A nonhuman?" The Ulsar seemed to be experiencing difficulty in getting used to the idea. "What's he like?"

Shangrin turned to Smirno.

"Why don't you describe him? After all, that's your specialty."

Smirno made a face but did not retort.

"He calls himself a Runi," he said. He described

the alien minutely, but he kept certain details to himself. He did not mention the highly developed tactical sense of the Runi, nor his extraordinary powers of perception. He did describe him as a furry crab endowed with a keen intelligence, which was, after all, accurate.

The Ulsar seemed to be thinking.

"He isn't dangerous?" he asked.

It was Shangrin who answered. "No, he's completely trustworthy. He has already been very useful."

"And what does he expect in exchange?"

"Nothing. It was scientific curiosity that made him accompany us."

"Oh!" said the Ulsar.

Shangrin poured the tea into little earthenware pots. The Ulsar tasted the burning liquid and made a face.

"The Runi belongs to your time period?"

"Yes," said Shangrin.

"Have you and his species been on good terms for a long time?"

I could lie, Shangrin thought, but what good would that do?

"We were the first to come into contact with his planet."

"I see," said the Ulsar.

He swallowed some more tea.

"I prefer wine."

"Tea is less harmful."

"To what period in time do you belong?"

This could be a harmless question, but Smirno made a mental note of it. What meaning could a date have to the Ulsar?

"The year 27,937 of our era," said Shangrin, "roughly two hundred and thirty million years from now. Naturally, all sorts of adjustments have to be made. Time does not elapse in the same manner on board an interstellar ship as it does in the worlds which it visits."

"I know that," said the Ulsar.

He seemed inexplicably relieved.

"I think that the origin of our people is located in your future," he went on. "The legends are vague, but

you are situated very near the beginning of the era. The
first ships that landed on Xandra must have come from
two or three hundred thousand years in your future.
The ships of the oppressors came from an even more
remote future."

"So we are, in a way, your ancestors," said Shangrin.

"Regression has smoothed out the differences. Actually you are more advanced than we are. Time is so
complex."

"Do you think that some of those who drifted in here
crossed the time barrier of their own free will?"

The Ulsar raised his eyebrows.

"You want to know if there's any chance of your
getting back to your own period in time. Well, yes.
It's a faint one, but it does exist."

"As long as we fight on your side, is that it?"

The Ulsar smiled. "Maybe. You're awfully suspicious."

"I'm used to deals."

"You're right."

The Ulsar closed his eyes and his face suddenly
looked old and tired. Deep lines were etched on his
forehead. His cheeks had become hollow. He was flinch-
ing under the burden of his responsibilities. Normally
he wore a mask of confidence and energy, but he had
just taken it off, in front of strangers.

"We're just toys," he said. "How do you account for
the fact that so many ships have been thrown back into
the past and were stranded here?"

"We have no precise information," said Shangrin.
"It was very sudden in our case. It was pure chance
that we even realized what happened. As I see it, there
are two possibilities: it could be a natural phenomenon,
a whirlwind almost unimaginable in its magnitude which
swallows up ships at some point in the continuum and
hurls them into another point of that continuum. Ele-
mentary particles are occasionally subject to such phe-
nomena, but on an infinitely reduced scale."

The Ulsar shook his head.

"But we have another theory," Shangrin went on.

"We think that in some fabulously distant future there is a race which has mastered the secret of time. We believe it's juggling with our ships, projecting them into the past or into the future, either to protect itself or to carry out a plan about which we know nothing. It may even be a game. This stellar region seems to be a privileged place: so many ships at several centuries' intervals have ended up here. Since the masters of time treat us like pawns, they must be anxious, whatever their plan, to control our movements. It must be possible to make contact with them, perhaps even negotiate with them."

"They really do exist," said the Ulsar. "I'm sure of that. And I think they are in direct contact with some of the empires around us. I am not sufficiently high in my group to know exactly what it covers, but in the early days it did receive help from secret organizations. Even today we still receive, via a complex chain of intermediaries, weapons that no one in this region of space could possibly manufacture. And out in space there is talk of gods, powerful entities in shadowy grottoes who can shape history. The Empire, for its part, receives other support. It's as though another struggle—an invisible one—was taking place behind the facade of our war, perpendicular to our space, on the battlefield of time."

Shangrin leaned toward him.

"Have you any proof?"

"Yes," said the Ulsar, "I do. But I must reach an agreement with you before I give it to you."

"Out of the question," objected Shangrin. "I buy only what I see."

"Listen," said the Ulsar, "if we defeat Xandra, if the federation is achieved, if my organization wins out, you may be able to follow the leads I will mention to you, perhaps even reach the masters of time. Faced with an upheaval, they might show themselves. They're very near. It may be your own chance."

"I want to see," Shangrin persisted.

"Very well." The Ulsar seemed to have come to a

decision. "I'm going to tell you a secret that no one on this planet except me has any idea of. You'll make up your mind when you've seen it. I'm almost sure what your answer will be."

He got up and raised the hanging over the door. The fatigue on his face had vanished, replaced by a strange smile pulling at the corners of his mouth.

"Follow me," he said, plunging into the night.

The camp slept. Torches spattered the darkness along the walls; silent watchmen glided along the edges of the palisades. At the end of a row of tents, a wavering voice sang, echoed by a drunken group. An occasional bark or the long sonometric howling of a hexapod tore through the night.

The tent behind them was like a dark monolithic mass. On the square, they could make out the shapes of gliders whose polished metal caught flickering reflections. Inside, men from the Magellanics slept and guards kept their watch.

The Ulsar clapped. An armed giant stepped out of the shadows.

"Take a torch and follow me," said the Ulsar.

The giant did so.

"We have searchlights," said Shangrin.

"No good. Anyway, I shall need him."

They went across the field under the dancing light of the torch. It revealed the clashing colors of the tents and the banners stuck in the ground. The sounds of soft voices reached them, but there was absolute calm and peace. The Ulsar's discipline must have been pitiless. Or perhaps his soldiers, inured to the long tyranny of the Empire, had never lost the habit of going to ground at night. The Magellanites saw weapons that were in startling contrast to the armor and swords of the warriors—long rockets. Although they were not the product of a high degree of technology, they could not have been manufactured in Xandra, except, perhaps, in the cities.

"Have you ever captured any arsenals of the Empire?"

The Ulsar turned toward Shangrin.

"No, almost never. They explode as soon as we get in. These rockets come from space, but they are useless against the cities—their screens are impenetrable."

Smirno studied the man who carried the torch. He had harsh features and massive bones. Where did rockets fit in his primitive universe? For him, the explosion of atoms could only mean the rattle of divine swords: the gods fought above his head. He helped them as best he could, but had no illusions.

What's the difference between him and us? Smirno wondered. Above our heads . . .

There were stars, and the stars held mysterious entities who had mastered time.

They were quietly going down toward the bottom of the crater. Their footsteps made stones roll. Shangrin, very much on the alert, thought that this crater was in an odd position strategically. Its sides were not sufficiently high to hide the camp from sight or protect it from direct hits. They must, in fact, have made it perfectly visible from space. Then he remembered that he had seen nothing, suspected nothing, which was strange. The camp might have escaped human observation, but the computers should have picked it up. One more mystery.

The crater was not circular and its walls, dark edges against a light sky, were of uneven height. They were much higher in the direction toward which the men were headed. The crater was in the shape of an asymmetric ellipse. One end, where the walls were low, was wide and round. The other end was narrow and pointed and the raised rock was like a spur. It was at the end of this spur that the crater plunged into the planet's crust.

Although certain fragments seemed to have been vitrified by tremendous heat, the rock was not in the least lava-like, nor even like a granite outflow. The walls of the crater were not of volcanic origin, but were made of the same sedimentary deposits as the surrounding plain.

It appeared as though a monstrous projectile had struck the surface of the planet at an angle of just a few degrees, almost tangentially. As the meteor—or whatever—had penetrated the ground, it had dug up layers of rock piling them up in front of it, forming a spur; it had hurled other mounds of excavated material behind it.

The slope became steeper and they had to slow down. The soldier hesitated and stopped; the Ulsar took the torch from him. Terror and respect were mirrored in the large man's face. Shangrin guessed that these emotions were aroused by something more than the person of the Ulsar.

"We are going to see the gods," said the Ulsar to the warrior.

The other's face lighted up.

"I shall cross the threshold of heaven," he said in a rasping voice. "Thank you, oh thank you, Liberator."

He flung himself down on his knees and kissed the Ulsar's hands in front of the astounded Magellanites.

"Forward," said the Ulsar.

The man got up, took back the torch and went off with a lighter step. They passed a low barrier made of white stones that shone in the starlight. There must have been some taboo on the unguarded depths of the crater, like a forbidden frontier. The credulity of the barbarians made an inviolable temple of it.

The path was dug into the crater along a spiral that hugged the walls. On their right, the bottom of the crater was a shadowy chasm. Did it shrink down into the size of a well? Gregory wondered. Had the Ulsar finally set his trap, against all their expectations? His hand automatically slipped into his pocket and caressed the butt of a weapon.

Soon the spur loomed high over them as they moved under the rock overhang. In the torchlight they could see stratifications like a signature of fire; awesome energies had been unleashed for the space of a flash. The crater suddenly disappeared under them in the wall at an oblique angle. They remained suspended along the narrow path between the mountain and a circular abyss so vast that the light of the torch died before reaching the other side. Gregory resisted the temptation to turn on his searchlight and direct it at the bottom.

CHAPTER IX

. The path narrowed down until they had to walk in single file. The warrior went first, lighting up the shadows with his torch. The Ulsar followed with a light step. Shangrin went next, then Smirno, who was having a hard time keeping up. Gregory brought up the rear. As they plunged deeper into the crater, the stars disappeared one by one.

The barbarian and the Ulsar stopped at a point where the path seemed to widen and end. Shangrin's eyes searched the darkness, unable to see on the side of the chasm anything to explain the purpose of the expedition.

The Ulsar turned toward the rocky side; the Magellanites now saw that a narrow passage had been dug under the mountain. It was walled in by a heavy, crudely rounded block.

The barbarian put his torch into a fissure in the rock; trails of smoke on the stone were proof that others had been there before them. He put his entire weight against the rock, as the Ulsar instructed him. It hardly budged.

It was a strange sort of door, Shangrin thought, surprised that the Ulsar had not provided another one. Then he noticed that the stone, despite its natural appearance, fitted the passage like a key in a lock. It would have required powerful explosives to move it unless one knew exactly where to push and in what direction: rudimentary but efficient.

The stone finally pivoted, almost soundlessly. It barely moved, then found a new balance. A gentle push with a finger would suffice to return it to its original position. At a sign from the Ulsar, the warrior went into the subterranean passage and the rest followed him wordlessly.

The tunnel wound down steeply. It had apparently been dug out of the mountain rather crudely, for the traces of tools were still visible on the wall: they were like thousands of insect tracks.

It was warm. The men sniffed the air, detecting an odor of ozone. Were there power installations, a factory below?

The torch-bearer stopped suddenly. Shangrin very nearly ran into the Ulsar as a fresh wind brushed his cheek. The soldier raised the torch and the men saw below them a subterranean chamber, large and dark, probably the bottom of the crater. Titanic forces must have been unleashed in the heart of the hill for, here and there, the rock had crystallized and caught reflections of light from the flame. Smirno realized that he had seen other deep caverns like this one—caverns which had resulted from the explosion of stellar bombs lodged in the crust of a planet.

They all stood at the edge of an abyss from which no light emanated; there was only a gentle breeze, like a current brushing against the walls of the grotto, which went out through the gaping mouth of the crater, into the depths below.

"Throw away your torch," the Ulsar said to the soldier.

Shangrin was about to protest, but he decided the Ulsar knew what he was doing. He was more at their mercy than they were at his. The torch went down, slowly, like a flower, and whirled about as the flame spread in the wind of its fall.

They thought it would continue to drop endlessly, but far, far below, a twin light came on, like a reflection in a looking glass, and the looking glass lighted up slowly, like a fire that is catching, and until the light owed nothing more to the torch. A soft bluish stain was spreading, like waves consuming the darkness. The walls of the chamber were already emerging from the

night. The light reached the edges and showed fallen
stones and the torch, burning itself out. They could see,
next to the torch, tiny, whitish objects.

The warrior threw himself on his knees.

"Look," said the Ulsar.

Then the man muttered unintelligible words that
seemed imbued with fervor. All this took place before
the Magellanites could make a single gesture.

The Ulsar pulled a sharp stiletto from his belt and
plunged it quickly and expertly into the nape of the
barbarian's neck. The man crumpled up without a
sound. The Ulsar extracted the weapon and blood
began to flow—very little. The Ulsar shoved his victim
into the crater and the body struck the fallen rock with
a sickening sound. The Magellanites saw what the
whitish objectes were: human bones. From that distance they looked like the remains of insects. There
were a great many.

The Ulsar sacrificed one of his men at each visit.
("We have a war to win.") A shiver ran up and down
Shangrin's spine. So the Ulsar was a liberator, was he?

The Magellanite did not protest. He knew it would
have been useless, and he was too experienced in the
ways of worlds and men. Besides, the Ulsar would not
have understod his indignation. It had been a natural,
obvious gesture for him, entirely without cruelty. The
secret had to be kept, that was all. And perhaps the
rebel from Xandra had wanted to demonstrate to the
spacemen the importance of the secret he was revealing
to them.

An enormous oblong object rested on the bottom of
the cavern—a spaceship. It might have fallen from the
stars one century or one millennium ago; it had made
the atmosphere hiss and roar with a red wake of fire
and a white foam of steam, and it had perforated the
ground, digging the crater, throwing earth hundreds of
yards up, clearing a passage for itself toward its final
resting place, its prison.

The shock must have been a violent one—the object
had traveled at least three hundred meters under the

surface of the planet before finally stopping and letting the torrents of unleashed energy spend themselves— but the object had sustained no visible damage. There was not the smallest knick, the slightest scratch along its surface. The most durable of the Lesser Magellanics' cruisers, under similar circumstance, would have been reduced to a few shards of scattered metal.

"May we go down?" asked Shangrin.

The Ulsar nodded and smiled sardonically. He leaned over the edge of the abyss, took a deep breath and jumped. He remained suspended for a brief moment, a dark spot above that lake of bluish light, then went down slowly toward the bottom, like a spider on the end of its thread.

Halfway down, he looked up and signaled them to follow.

"An anti-gravitational field," whispered Shangrin.

"I'll go first," Gregory suggested.

He hesitated briefly, then jumped. He saw the bluish stain rise up so fast that he thought he was going to crash, that he had to save himself. Then his fall was suddenly halted; he remained suspended in the air, as if he had run into an invisible elastic mattress. He looked up and saw the outlines of Shangrin and Smirno silhouetted against the dark rock. He immediately began to rise back up slowly and jerkily: subconsciously he had wanted to be close to them.

Below, the Ulsar was making strange signs. Gregory struggled against the fear that was invading him and thought: I want to go down. His theory was proved correct. He went down slowly and came to rest on the blue surface.

He saw that Shangrin was calling to him, but the captain's voice was muffled as it reached him; it was shapeless, unintelligible. The microradio was no longer functioning either, as the alien ship was surrounded by a halo of energy that disturbed the order of physical laws. The perfection of the anti-gravitational mechanism was unbelievable: its functioning was geared to the thinking of whoever wanted to reach the machine.

Gregory deduced from this that its builders must be
human, or at least not too different from those of his
own race. The machine's detectors must be capable of
recognizing and registering infinitesimal muscular con-
tractions and discharges of nervous influx.

It was likely that the apparatus did not entirely rely
on the principle of telepathy, but that it limited itself
to interpreting orders given by the entire nervous system
of the body to go up or come down or even move
laterally. It did not try to deal with problems posed by
the use of the words *up* or *down*. Consequently, any
being more or less like a human could use it. Perhaps
even a superior animal.

Gregory wondered what would happen if the Runi
were introduced to the machine. He wanted to go back
up to explain to Shangrin what had happened, but
the two men were already coming down at moderate
speed.

The Ulsar, from the other side of the cavern, was
signaling to them to come close so they started to slide
along the rounded, smooth surface. It was not uni-
formly blue, but showed something like a network of
small veins, some lighter, some darker than the background, and constantly changing so rapidly that the
eyes registered the phenomenon as a flutter. The cavern
more or less complemented the shape of the ship. In
some places, rock touched the blue hull and in others,
a gaping passage remained free. Toward the rear, the
vault was low and apparently prevented any exit through
the crater. Probably a fall of stones had blocked the
way.

"How long has this been here?" asked Gregory.

"Not very long," said Smirno. "Otherwise the crater
would be stopped up and its walls eroded. A few dozen
years at most. Probably less."

The voice carried badly, as if the air were too thick.
Radiation curtailed the vibrations. The space was
glutted with energy.

The Ulsar gestured that he wanted to take them
inside. They reached the opposite wall of the cavern

and went down by a passage dug out of the rock. They moved along the gigantic hull like so many worms along a fruit, looking for a place to get in to suck the juice. An oval opening appeared, breaking the uniform surface of the hull. It opened to a narrow corridor bathed in green light. They entered and crossed bare, mysterious rooms, lined with empty niches. The men guessed they might be means of transportation and communication, transmitting posts or launching pads permitting instant projection from one point to another in the ship, or perhaps to the outside, to other corresponding niches scattered throughout the cities and ships of an unimaginable civilization. The ceilings of the rooms were covered with mobile, luminous designs that opened with jerky pulsations, then slowly vanished only to reappear. Nowhere did they find instruments or instrument panels, levers, weapons, quadrants, books, logs, detectors. But looking for them was probably as futile for them, Shangrin thought, as for a barbarian from a heroic period to look in the *Vasco* for a sail, a sextant, a tiller, a rudder.

This ship had traveled in time; not only in space. It was as different from the *Vasco* as the *Vasco* was from a sailboat.

They soon finished exploring the open passages, certainly less than one-hundreth of the ship's total mass, without seeing a trace of a door that might lead to the rest. And Shangrin had no illusions about the possibility of breaking down the partitions: the ship's resistance exceeded the properties of matter. It was the result of certain subtle alterations of space, perhaps even of time. In fact, these two aspects of things were inextricably linked here.

When they had finished exploring they stopped in a vast triangular room whose walls must have been imperceptibly curved, for the angles were wider than prescribed by Euclidean geometry. In addition, the ribs of the room seemed to be in a continuous flow which side-tracked and tired the eye. The Ulsar stretched and floated up. The Magellanites instantly followed suit, merely thinking their desire. There was no necessity for constant effort to continue floating, once was sufficient.

"There you are," said the Ulsar. "This ship appeared from nowhere a few years after my arrival on this world. At the time I was in another section of the planet and the news took a long time to reach me. I didn't immediately realize its importance. Neither, for that matter, did the cities, for they made only feeble efforts to locate it and they did not succeed."

He stared at them, wearing his customary smile.

"Yet the shock had been extraordinarily violent. It was heard for miles and miles around—it had shaken the ground. But the crater remained unnoticed by the squadrons of the Empire. *I* found it because I was moving slowly, close to the ground, instead of soaring proudly in the air."

He pivoted. This made the men feel slightly uneasy, and vaguely disquieted. The Ulsar seemed perfectly at home here despite his barbaric garb. He was the owner. Shangrin strode out aggressively, face to face with him, as though he had conquered the ship, but he was still an outsider. He was sure of his strength, of his rights, he did not feel remotely intimidated, but he was still an outsider. Gregory was no more than his shadow. He would doubtless accomplish great things in the future, for his mind was open, but he lacked the weight of maturity. As for Smirno, he was only a curious, weary, and sometimes vindictive onlooker, a recorder. It was in an alien place like this, outside of time, that personalities stood out most clearly, that the details of humdrum existence vanished, allowing the naked substance of the being to show through. An almost imperceptible aura surrounded Shangrin. An equally faint green light that matched the walls of the room bathed the Ulsar. Gregory and Smirno had no lights.

"The crater is not visible from the sky," the Ulsar went on. "That was all. And what was underground could not be detected. Some sort of contraption enclosed the space on itself, deflected light rays. I don't know about those things. You know them better than I do. As one approaches along the ground, on certain days, as one gets nearer the crater, there is a noticeable shimmering of air that is attributed to heat. But it is no such thing. It is a contraction of space and perhaps of time.

"Slaves who had run away from the cities had taken refuge in the crater. They had nóticed the Empire ships stopped pursuing them when they arrived here. Much later, I learned why. From the sky, only a continuous plain is visible. This may be an image of the past held prisoner by this machine and eternally projected above it like a shield against the passage of time. But, at the time, I could only see two things: the enigma and the potential power that this ship represented, and the asylum which the crater offered."

"Has it remained inviolate?" asked Shangrin.

"Yes. Twice we had to wipe out ground expeditions from the Empire which had ventured too close, probably by chance. They were only insignificant patrols and the cities did not undertake any searches. They had enough to do on other fronts."

"And the ship was accessible?"

"No. When I arrived, the crater had already become a sacred place. A religion was taking hold. The fugitives who lived here believed in the protection of the gods. Some of them had gone to the bottom of the crater and had seen a blue, supernatural light through the cracks. Some had tried to reach it. They never came back.

"I discovered what had happened to them—they had reached the stern of the ship. There is a violent blue whirlwind there which defies description. It is not very large, and it is insubstantial, but it is fatal to anyone who touches it or even comes close to it. I've seen it swallow men whole. It's something like a blind, voracious god. I think of it as the incarnation of time. There, seconds are counted, ground up and destroyed. Anyone who plunges into the whirlwind is projected into the ultimate future or the absolute past, or into emptiness. I had the crater plugged up with rocks, and this path dug out. I've discovered a few things about this ship, but

I don't know where it came from, nor when, nor what civilization built it. I'm positive that it was conceived by man, or at least for men. I think it comes from a distant future because nowhere, in the space around us, is there comparable technology. And we know that one can be propelled involuntarily out of the future. My theory is that this ship came voluntarily, that there was an accident and its crew disappeared; the ship ran into the planet by chance, by a miscalculation in its course that brought it too close to the planet. There are other possibilities. I don't know. Only the silence is discernible. But this ship is full of knowledge; I often come here to think. My people say that I come here to listen to the gods, that I am the only one allowed to come back from the underworld. Look at the ceiling."

They did so. The ceiling at first looked smooth except for the more or less luminous network palpitating under its surface; then it gradually became crowded with shapes, colored, intertwined, superimposed shadows. They clashed, then dissolved into a kaleidoscopic succession of abstract events. It could have been no more than an illusion, the result of optic fatigue, but it was too real. There was an innate logic at work which the mind could perceive without understanding. Could it be writing, or perhaps mathematics?

"I understand some of the series," said the Ulsar. "How can I explain? This has made a new man of me; it has altered my thinking, made it disciplined, clearer. Perhaps there's no meaning really, or maybe it's a map of time, the shifting, interlacing of inaccessible roads connecting periods in time. Perhaps it's really only a game. But at least this helps me better understand those who built this ship."

His voice grew louder. It was devoid of passion, but it became more vibrant, more urgent.

"And what this ship has done, others can do again more successfully. I think some of them are sailing in the space around us. I believe that when our power has become sufficiently great, they will make contact with us or they will no longer slip through the meshes of our net. They are very near, there, behind the web of things."

"Could I bring my technicians here?" Shangrin asked.

The Ulsar shook his head.

"Their instruments won't work. I've brought scientists here from the cities, prisoners. They were so eager to solve this mystery that they would have done anything, even remained here, had they been given the chance. They were unable to find a clue. I had to have them killed.

"So there's your proof. The road to the future does exist. This is a lock—now find the key."

"We'll find it in victory," said Shangrin. "Ulsar, I'm with you. We'll take the cities. We'll liberate space. We'll bend time to our will."

"Time is an inconstant ally and an eternal foe," said the Ulsar with a smile.

Having left the ship, they retraced their footsteps along the rocky path and reentered the tunnel. After they had rounded the first bend, the blue light grew dim and went out. As they left the cavern, they climbed back into darkness because their searchlights did not work; just as well, for their eyes needed to rest before facing the brightness of a dawning sky. And so they left the cavern of night.

CHAPTER X

Rockets were raining down on a city named Tczila. From the Magellanite's headquarters, they looked like a volley of silver arrows. They shot out from the mountains in clusters, climbed so high in the atmosphere that no sound betrayed their upward passage and then aimed, hissing, at the town.

But the rockets never reached the city. At a few kilometers' altitude, they ran into an invisible obstacle and exploded. Radiation and heat glanced off the energy rampart that protected the city. Sunlight filtered through, however; Shangrin could see clearly, through his field glasses, heavy, massive buildings. The rocket explosions created clouds which were slowly dispersed by the wind, that was all. Not enough for Tczila to worry about.

This was why the outcome of the war was still in doubt. The rebellions of the plains beat upon the walls of the city like the waves of a stormy sea, but were powerless against the fortifications. The soldiers of the Empire were not sufficiently numerous to control all of the plains, nor were they equipped to do so. The opposing sides came face to face only by prearrangement, and the war had lasted so long that these meetings had become rare and uncertain.

To be sure, one or two cities had fallen as the result of internal revolts. But Tczila was sheltered from these tremors: the skulls of suspect slaves served as decorations for the gruesome pyramids at the gates.

And that was why, Shangrin said to himself, swords had survived the advent of rockets, why hand-to-hand combat, the bow and arrow and the cavalry had outlasted weapons of massive destruction, rays, gliders and tanks. He could see, through his field glasses, the columns of the Ulsar as they made their way toward the city. His own men were ready to intervene with primitive arms that hurled projectiles instead of disintegrating rays. The latter was a technique that had completely escaped the Ulsar and the Empire and which might have been enough to transform the war, if it had worked.

From the very beginning, Shangrin had been opposed to the direct use of the *Vasco*; he wanted to keep his ship uninvolved as long as possible. He had put only his skill and combat troops at the service of the Ulsar.

The Magellanites' customary weapons had proved to be inoperative. The field that protected the city had made them explode. Shangrin had listened skeptically to the Ulsar's explanations until the rebel had ordered a march on the city with his barbarians carrying nuclear grenades and radiant pistols. They had vanished without so much as a flame. Shangrin had grown livid, but had not belabored the issue. The Ulsar's demonstrations were always to the point.

And yet he was not inhuman, Smirno thought now, as he watched with the liveliest interest preparations for the battle. This was the first time he had witnessed a battle from such close quarters. It was also probably the first time such strange armies confronted one another. The city was too far away for him to make out evidence of agitation amid its population, but every so often a group of barbarians would disappear in a cloud of smoke as one of the small rockets backfired.

Fires ravaged the fields. The besieged were using thermal rays. In the sky, flying low and protected by the invisible rampart, large black airplanes were circling like so many birds of prey. They were powerless, though. The city could not launch nuclear projectiles—the field would have exploded them as soon as they were launched. This was a curious war.

Gregory was waiting to give the signal to release the planelets. The strategic problem involved in the capture of the city boiled down, in the long run, to the neutralization of the energy rampart. The Ulsar could not bring it off but the *Vasco* technicians believed they had found the solution.

The field of protection was of a subnuclear type. It was made up of much less massive particles than those which normally accompanied electromagnetic vibrations, and, correlatively, the wavelength of the rays which set it in operation was much greater, somewhat on the order of intersiderial distances. Consequently, the energy level of the field was quite low, almost negligible. It worked only indirectly, by interrupting the structure of space and intervening at a subparticle level on the connection between matter and energy. This was enough to cause the explosion of nuclear arms and radiant pistols or their derivatives.

Paradoxically, the Magellanites were unable to produce that type of field—it was the result of a more technologically advanced era than theirs. But its generator was probably extremely simple, and this explained why the Empire had managed to safeguard its secret while having forgotten its principle.

The Magellanites could not cancel out the positive field by a negative one, but they could weaken it by draining energy from it. A simple antenna casts a shadow in an alternating electromagnetic field because it absorbs energy. In general, the consumption of energy thus salvaged on radio waves is negligible compared to the amount transmitted. But, in theory, it is possible to absorb all the energy.

The problem was simplified in the case of the subnuclear field because it had well-defined limits. Once past these limits, it decreased in proportion to a square of a square of the distance. It was practically annulled within a few centimeters.

Hence Operation Planelet.

Gregory studied the dial of his watch. It was shifting from yellow to red and numbers were appearing behind small shutters. These were signals from units announcing, one by one, that they were ready.

The dial turned black . . . Gregory gave an order.

Dozens of technicians, spaced all around Tczila, set off their contraptions.

Several million planelets, scarcely larger than birds, flew close to the ground toward the city, like a moving multicolored rug. With their long shining wings, they looked like a swarm of dragonflies.

They reached the energy field and immediately started to gain altitude. Horizontally, they never went closer to the field, but stayed exactly at its limit. As they climbed, they created an unwavering crown along the city's invisible protective field, some joined up at the top, forming a gleaming hemisphere that covered the city like a thick cloud of insects. Their metallic antennae drew off energy from the field itself and that energy kept the engines going. The planelets could fly as long as the field lasted, but they were weakening it considerably. In fact, almost all it could now do was refuel them. They sometimes collided, destroyed one another and fell in clusters, but there were millions of them and technicians kept sending in new flights.

The sky within the city must have been darkened by them. The psychologcal effect was not the least important factor.

A faint hiss startled Gregory, who turned to look. The Runi's egg was floating directly overhead. The primitive idea of the planelets had been his. The technicians and robots of the *Vasco* had carried it out, but he had found the solution to the problem as soon as it had been put to him. It was a theoretical solution: the Runi produced nothing, his civilization knew nothing about tools. He was a problem solver.

The protective egg had also been one of his inventions. He had decided he needed to be mobile in order to follow Shangrin. He had given the specifications for the contraption and the physicists of the *Vasco* had built it. The egg was completely transparent and hermetically sealed. It contained, besides the Runi, all the necessities of life for him and for communicating his thought into human language—including a chessboard set up right in front of him. An anti-gravitational generator allowed him to move in space. He looked, in his transparent egg, like an enormous orange larva, heavy with unforeseeable transformations.

The first rocket to cross the barrier of the planelets fell with a creaking of metal and exploded instantly, inside the city. It had crossed the wall of energy—the city was virtually destroyed. The Runi's tactic had worked.

But Gregory knew that things would not be quite so simple. The greater part of the installations must have been buried deep. Furthermore, there must be other parts of Tczila. An enormous cloud of smoke rose, shoving aside the planelets. The wings of a number of devices melted, others left the field and crashed after whirling around. When the cloud had been dissipated, only about a quarter of the planelets were still flying in the weakened field. They plummeted to the ground just as a second rocket roared by. For a second Gregory was able to believe that the first explosion had destroyed the field's generator, but the second rocket exploded in mid-air: the field had been reactivated. The last planelets had not yet touched the ground before they rose again. The field was again drained off and they fell, finally to the ground.

The defenders of Tczila took countermeasures. The Magellanites sent out another swarm, but they scarcely had time to mount an assault on the invisible hemisphere. Only one rocket out of a dozen got by.

"Men are dying," said the Runi.

It was a simple statement uttered in the Runi's synthetic monotone, devoid of warmth. It could have contained surprise or understanding or even compassion. Or else satisfaction.

A sudden violent hatred welled up inside Gregory because of that statement. Until that moment he had felt dispassionate about the events unfolding around him: the cloud of smoke, the giant mushroom which wafted, with no apparent reason, at an altitude of several kilometers. The Runi had brought him back to reality. There were men dying, not just the cruel citizens of the Empire, but their slaves also. He glanced at Shangrin. The captain did not seem to share his doubts. He was barking orders and carrying on as though the battle had been quite close.

"Synchronize the launching of rockets and the releasing of the swarms," said the Runi.

Of course, thought Gregory. He wasn't the only one who was thinking.

He gave brief orders. The rockets and the planelets flew off at irregular intervals. Most of the rockets exploded in mid-air, but a few got through. That was enough.

The city, ten kilometers away, was a bonfire.

It had become the core of a sun, a burning brazier, a heap of ashes; metal and stone fused, swimming in an ocean of steam.

From the scorched plains, columns of barbarians and Magellanites were marching on the city. The rockets stopped falling. The planelets that were still intact, returned to their launchers. Only a fraction of them remained.

The batle was virtually over and won although fighting would probably continue for several days in the underground of the city—battles between rats, of no importance. The most powerful city of the planet had been taken. For the first time in over a century, the balance of power had been destroyed. It had taken only three hours.

Shangrin jumped off his glider and rushed toward the Ulsar.

"Tonight the city will be in your hands," he shouted.

"I know how much I owe you," said the Ulsar. "But in the next battle, we'll have to try to save the ships of the stellar port. We'll need them later."

"We'll conquer space. No one can stop us."

No, no one, thought Smirno. We've roasted them in their dwellings like so much poultry. He felt weary, nauseated. He hated Shangrin's brutal joy, the icy impassivity of the Ulsar. He hated all men of war. The

sight of the bombs falling on the city had aroused feelings of cowardice within him.

When the men from the Magellanics and the rebels
of Xandra entered the city, wiping out erratic fires, they
were surprised at the manner in which the buildings of
Tczila had withstood the nuclear fallout. Light shadows
on burned walls bore witness to destroyed lives. Steel
and concrete had flowed in the streets in incandescent
rivers which were cooling off, but in the very heart of
Tczila, huge and blind buildings were still standing like
rocks. Their walls had taken on the polish of enamel;
their doors had all been soldered by the heat.

They searched all these caverns. In the bottom of one
of them they found a chained man who was still breathing. They carried him outside. He had just enough
strength to breathe, to say "Thank you." Then he died.

After that, they looked for doors leading to the underground shelters of the city, opened them, went down
and showed no quarter. The vronns had their work cut
out for them.

After Tczila, it was the turn of Azultl, then Xiotl,
Shipar and Nuss. The first two cities fell before the
Empire had made a concerted effort to regain control.
Then the cities undertook to support one another and
a few rare spaceships came to back them up. When one
was destroyed, the others fled; thereafter they limited
themselves to watching over the planet, releasing weapons to the cities now and then. Shangrin did not pursue
them; he had other things to do.

The cities fell one by one and of some of them there
remained only ashes, melted rock and a fine dust that
rose to the edge of space. It would take years for it to
fall down again. Others surrendered almost intact,
which spared many lives. The chains changed bearers.
On maps, the troops of the Ulsar and Shangrin were so
many colored trajectories which soon covered most of
the planet like a net. The Ulsar conquered other tribes
of barbarians. Once they crossed an ocean to take
revenge on a city that was showering rockets on them.

That took months. In its cavern, the ship from time continued to sleep. The *Vasco* had returned to space and orbited about Xandra. For those who did not take part in the war, it was as though their long voyage was being continued.

Men changed, or became even more set in their ways. The Ulsar was more enigmatic than ever, more unyielding, even more self-assured. There seemed to be no limit to his dreams. He wanted to carry the war into space and take the Empire in its capital as soon as possible. But Shangrin was not giving in to him; he tried to slow down the involvement of the Magellanites and to interfere as little as possible with the Ulsar's politics. After all, he was a businessman, not a power politician. Yet he liked victories. He was the first to enter a city once, sword in hand, at the head of a troop of barbarians. Fire and blood left him unmoved, but the death of a Magellanite put him into a black rage. He would demand his share of the loot, but would put it into the *Vasco's* common treasury. He was great in the manner of captains of old, half trader, half pirate.

This fascinated Gregory, who was nauseated by blood. He thought destruction pointless. He would have preferred getting there more slowly, more subtly, more cautiously.

But this was not an era when people were concerned with refinements, Smirno thought. It was a period when the strong reigned until the weak unexpectedly rebelled. Until this moment, he had contemplated from afar the rise and fall of civilizations, their struggles. In the end, massacres and fires were reduced to a few lines on a data slip. He thought he had a clear view and thorough understanding of that type of misfortune, past or future, but Xandra was something new; it was reality. He could hear the cries of anguish, smell the odor of smoke and rot. And there was no remedy. None. No one could persuade the Ulsar or Shangrin or the haughty officers of the Empire who approached death with an oath on their lips that they ought to play at other games than war. This bloodletting and devastation was destiny to

them. The enemy themselves were part of the con-
spiracy and Smirno hated them for this as much as he
hated the others. He began to hope for Shangrin's
downfall.

The Runi probably changed too, although no one
could be sure nor guess to what extent. The image of
man in the secret torrent of his thoughts evolved,
became clearer, without ever quite becoming set. The
Runi's point of view, all hatred aside, was singularly
like Smirno's. But whereas the xenologist was resigned
in his role as a spectator, each day the Runi saw more
clearly the threads that regulated those lives. The chessboard took up less and less of his time.

It was also in the nature of the Runi to play games
and he had discovered that the pleasure derived from
gaming was part of his own complexity.

Like happy children, they forced open the gates of
Cindra. It was an ancient city and its masters, who were
all too few, had offered little resistance. They had been
less cruel to their slaves than most of the citizens of
the Empire and the anger of the freed slaves had been
less violent than elsewhere. A spaceship, taking advantage of the confusion, escaped. Shangrin at least
marched straight to the port and his men were able to
search the old patrician houses before the arrival of the
barbarians. The libraries were crammed with books
which recorded details and recollections of the world
before the Passage. Those were the documents Shangrin
wanted to preserve.

They took the port almost without striking a blow.
Shangrin, with the help of Smirno, was examining the
captured ships when an old man who said he was a
historian was brought to him. He wore a green silk
tunic and appeared to be frightened and sick. Shangrin
shrugged when he saw him. Until then neither he nor
the Ulsar had succeeded in extracting information of
any use from the prisoners. The Empire was falling
apart too rapidly. The rulers of Xandra knew little of
what was happening on the other worlds, either because

communication was faulty or because the Empire had decided to abandon the planet to its fate, to circle Xandra with a sanitary cordon rather than recapture it. But what this man had to tell them changed everything.

"What's your name?" asked Shangrin.

"Hari Ilen Cindra," said the historian.

He belonged to the ruling family of the city, Shangrin thought, his interest aroused in spite of himself. The man seemed less arrogant than others of his caste, more open, more intelligent.

"What was your occupation?"

"I was studying history. It is a gloomy branch of learning. It allows one to foresee the defeats of the future in the victories of the past."

"Did you foresee your defeat?"

"Yes," said the historian. "I knew you'd come sooner or later."

"And you did nothing to warn your people?"

"I never stopped warning them, but they thought themselves masters of their fate. You think you're master of your fate too, but you're wrong."

"What do you mean?"

"My people believed that this was only a slaves' rebellion and that it could not succeed. They refused to believe that they were only pawns and that the real game was not being played at their level."

"Why are you telling me this?"

"Because you won't believe me. You see, our struggles, our Empire and our revolt are unimportant. They're only small clouds. They're only the ephemeral accidents of another war. We are not fighting for ourselves. We are struggling along an undefined front between two gigantic armies. I have noticed and observed many things during the course of years I've been examining the archives. I found strange things there, the story of entire nations displaced in time to pursue an endless war. I have guessed how the players will move the pawns."

"You spoke about time?"

"Yes. I don't know where you come from but you

don't belong to this world. Perhaps you come from the future. Perhaps you're only a mercenary, or even one of those who understand the other face of things. Perhaps I ought not to have spoken out."

Shangrin threw himself at the man, grabbed him by the throat and shook him.

"Explain yourself! I don't understand. I'm lost in time—I come from the future. Tell me what you know and I'll set you free."

"I've told you everything I know," said the historian. "Listen. Two great powers are fighting in time and space, but because of cowardice or exhaustion they confront one another only through intermediaries. They wrangle over planetary systems without risking a single man. All they do is send someone from place to place to set off a conflict; then someone in the opposing camp does the same thing and war starts. There is death and destruction. The line of demarcation between the powers wavers and fluctuates. The field of battle moves. We had such a man confronting us."

"Not I," said Shangrin.

He had almost shouted it out.

"Then look for him. Perhaps he is in your retinue, but he used you to defeat us. He is your real master."

"I don't believe it," said Shangrin.

But he was not so sure. They had taken and burned cities, found documents, questioned officers, followed clues, studied the organization of the empire; the Ulsar's promises had been empty. They had fought this war for nothing. Men and time had been lost and now this historian from Cindra claimed they had been used . . . perhaps by the Ulsar.

Ever since they had left their own time, the shadows of great powers had floated over them. Gregory had supposed they existed, the Ulsar had proved it. And now this man . . . A flash of despair ran through Shangrin. The Xandra war was no more than the feverish activity of an anthill. Perhaps they had purposely been precipitated from the future in order to wipe out the Empire, to alter a delicate balance of forces. He took a longer look at the historian who answered his un-spoken question.

"We lost because the gods abandoned us. They withdrew. We had become worthless to them. The front moved; a few thousand worlds are going to change masters in one move. Then the struggle will start all over again, step by step."

"But why?" asked Shangrin. "Why this struggle?"

"I don't know," said the historian. Perhaps for fun."

"For fun," the Runi's voice echoed mechanically.

The transparent egg was over them. The Runi had listened to the man from Cindra. Then he left.

Shangrin had almost forgotten this interrogation as city after city fell and burned and revealed nothing, not the thinnest track to lead them back to the future, to their own world. The conversation had left a small impression, however, an indefinable feeling of unease. His recollection of it woke up all at once, grew light, opened like a flower when the Ulsar was killed.

It was just at the end of the war, after they had returned to the field where the crater was. For several days the Ulsar had been urging the Magellanites to go into space. Shangrin was torn between weariness of the war and ambition: the thought of founding an empire went to his head like wine, then he would forget the future and Neo-Sirius and Lorne. The moment seemed propitious.

The Ulsar had become increasingly demanding, even insolent. He had, he said, the means to attack the Empire alone if Shangrin did not want to follow him. He was alternatively ingratiating and threatening.

The Runi, Shangrin and the Ulsar were alone in the Ulsar's tent. The Runi was silent, but suddenly, at a turn in the discussion, he said to the Ulsar: "I know now who you are."

And almost simultaneously he turned to Shangrin and gave an order.

"Kill him."

The Ulsar made a move, but Shangrin reacted at

once. His weapon barked and the Ulsar fell to the ground. His clenched fingers still held a minute radiance.

It all happened so fast that for a long time after Shangrin wondered why he had acted as he did. Perhaps the Runi held a hypnotic power over him. Then he told himself how in this brutal act, the hatred for the Ulsar that had slowly been growing up inside him had erupted. It was made up of a thousand facts, doubts, hunches; it went back also to the words of the historian, to secret knowledge behind the Ulsar's mask which concealed more than the details of a revolution.

The Ulsar did not die at once.

"I made a mistake," said the Runi. "I ought never to have told you to kill him here. When he dies, the ship buried under the hill will explode. A mechanism in that ship is tuned to his life. I didn't know. I've only just discovered it."

"The ship is his?"

"Yes," said the Runi. "I've known almost since the start. He isn't a pawn on the chessboard. Nor even a madman. He is one of the players."

"One of the players?"

The Ulsar was breathing with difficulty. Bloodstained foam oozed from his lips. Shangrin saw that he was trying to speak.

"We must get out," the Runi said.

Shangrin wanted to help the wounded man, lift him up, take him along or summon help.

"No," said the Runi. "There isn't time. In any event he must die."

As they left the tent it seemed to Shangrin that the Ulsar was smiling in a sinister way. Stunned, the Magellanite automatically followed the transparent egg. The sharp outside air brought him to and he shouted out orders. His men rushed to the gliders and the aircraft soon took off toward the south. Shangrin looked at the barbarians, then at the walls made of earth and grass. The palisades hid the tents. All at once he sensed the Ulsar's passage over the threshold of death, for inside he felt as though a page in his existence had been torn up. Now everything was clear. He knew the Ulsar had tricked him from the very start, just as he had taken advantage of the barbarians; he did indeed belong to that breed who were the masters of time, who played with men as with pawns on a chessboard. Shangrin acknowledged that the foreign ship from the future could not, despite its fantastic resistance, have withstood the tremendous shock of impact—the crater was only a camouflage. But Shangrin had not made these discoveries, even though all this information had been accumulating in his subconscious over a long period of time.

It was the Runi who had provided the key. The Runi—a better chess player than Shangrin—held in his absurd limbs the elements of another round of this game. Suddenly Shangrin hated the entire universe. He understood the Ulsar's smile and the "for fun" of the historian, for his life now held no other purpose than to conquer and destroy in the impossible hope of reaching the hidden players and making them pay for the game.

"What happened?" asked Gregory.

"I've killed the Ulsar," said Shangrin.

At that very moment the spur was slowly lifted and a thin red streak appeared at its base; it looked as though it was going to remain balanced there for an eternity and that these questions were no longer important. Then they distinctly saw the rock splinter; there was a great flash of light, and space and time were chopped and mixed and a ball of fire sprang from the ground. They threw themselves down in the bottom of the gliders, their eyes watering and reflecting red lights. The wind caught up two of the gliders and dashed them to the ground.

The others miraculously escaped. Lava rose from the depths of the earth and filled the new crater.

CHAPTER XI

He had aged, but it only made him more awe-inspiring, Gregory thought as he came before Shangrin. Now it was as if there was a gap between him and the rest of the world, as if his words and deeds were of another period. He was living like a barbarian among barbarians. His beard was not as well kept as it used to be.

It would be difficult to get him to accept the fact that the passengers of the *Vasco* had had enough of war and Shangrin's absurd and endless quest. Up there in space, in the company of Norma, the thirst for conquest seemed alien, monstrous. Everything seemed so peaceful in the spherical ship. A smell of spring floated in the ersatz parks. Here, it smelled of leather, oil and metal.

"Well?" said Shangrin.

"They want you to stop. They demand your return and the gliders'. They say you'll never stop. They request a meeting of the committee and a restatement of policy."

Shangrin got up. He moved slowly, hesitantly now. The bear inside him was tired.

"I've told you, Gregory, to let them know what my decisions are; you are not to take orders or advice from them. I know what I must do."

Gregory stiffened.

"They are not barbarians," he said. "They won't obey blindly. They are threatening to break off all contact with you, to cut off your supplies."

"I'll get along without them. I have my own fleet— thirty-two magnificent ships armed to the gunwales. I can defeat an armada from the Empire, destroy its capital, capture the entire system."

Gregory stiffened some more.

"I'm afraid you don't quite understand, captain. You are here alone. The exploration teams will probably follow you, but without the ship, you're lost."

Shangrin's head turned slowly, as if moved by an independent mechanism. Silver threads had slipped into his beard and hair and his face had become deeply furrowed. His eyes were now less deeply set.

He raised his powerful hands as if to curse the passengers of the *Vasco*; Gregory noticed they were shaking slightly.

"Alone," grumbled Shangrin. "The Ulsar was alone and just look at what he accomplished. Everyone is alone. I'm not afraid of being alone."

"They're talking of calling in the guardians."

"I'm not afraid of the guardians. I'm not afraid of anyone. I'm even willing to challenge the masters of time. I have thirty-two spaceships; I'm going to attack them and reduce them to dust."

The Magellanites had given Gregory the authority to arrest Shangrin and bring him on board the *Vasco*. They had decided the captain was mad, and Gregory believed they were right. But he couldn't do it. After all, he was Shangrin the lone wolf, Shangrin the bear, Shangrin the Great. And Gregory thought of Norma. He told himself that if he didn't make his choice now, he never would. He had worked with this man, undergone hardships with him. Shangrin had been like a father to him and now something strange had happened to him, had broken him. The cracks were visible; Shangrin was no longer himself since the Ulsar's death.

"I'll never be alone," said Shangrin. "I have the Runi with me. And that's why you're handling me with gloves, isn't it? You're afraid of the Runi, all of you."

Gregory did not answer. It was true. Smirno had urged caution because of the Runi, because of the strange bond between a mad old man, obsessed with dreams of power, and a nonhuman of infinite intelli-

gence. The others on the *Vasco* had sneered, but Smirno
had recalled them to prudence and he, Gregory, was
afraid.

Shangrin's triumphant laugh suddenly stopped.

'I killed the Ulsar," he said. "You know that, don't
you? I have forgotten why I killed the Ulsar."

His voice dragged woefully, then it rose, took on a
new resonance.

"Did you tell them that I killed the Ulsar? I was
walking in a labyrinth like a blind man and the truth
was there, burning brightly before my eyes, like a flame.
And I put it out. Oh, why did I kill the Ulsar? He was
my brother."

"Take it easy," said Gregory.

He took the old man by the arm, but Shangrin
pushed him back violently.

"I had to kill the Ulsar. He was tricking me, wasn't
he? Don't you see that we are all walking in darkness
and that I want to destroy it, burn it with my war fleet?
Do they want to die in the past, those people up there
in the *Vasco*?"

"They want peace. They're talking of establishing a
colony on a virgin planet."

"The Runi told me to kill him, so I did. I wouldn't
have gotten anything out of him anyway."

Smirno had told Gregory that if he couldn't persuade
the captain to come back, he should stay with him, trying to keep his trust. He had instructed Gregory to
hurry up, but not take any chances.

"I see," said Gregory.

"We have to continue the struggle. The universe must
be conquered, we must clear a path to the masters of
time."

"There is no other solution," said Gregory, giving in.

"We'll give you three months," Smirno had said. "If
you haven't brought him back by then, we'll take steps."

"What steps?" he had asked.

"We'll try to destroy the Runi and bring Shangrin
back on board the ship."

"He'll fight."

"Then we'll kill him."

"You're mad."

"No," Smirno had corrected, "he's mad."

"Who is the leader of the opposition on board the *Vasco*? Henrik?"

"No," answered Gregory, "Smirno."

"They're wrong. They're wrong. With the help of the Runi, we'll cross the threshold of time. I knew you'd remain faithful, Gregory. Tomorrow, tomorrow, our ships will go back into space. In one month, the Empire will be ours."

He would do it, there wasn't a shadow of doubt, and Gregory had no way of stopping him. The barbarians were loyal to him. He had told them that the Ulsar had died in the bombing of the field held by the fleets of the Empire and they had believed him. With the help of the rebels and the *Vasco* technicians who also remained faithful to him, he might succeed. He might just conquer the Empire. But it didn't make sense. It was like the blind work of a giant mole, digging in the ground, stretching out its domain in the night, aimlessly. He was a machine gone berserk.

They vanquished the fleet of the Empire in the vicinity of a triple sun. They lost fourteen ships but the Empire's armada, which had been three times as big as the Magellanites' at the start of the battle, was almost entirely destroyed in the raging floods of unleashed energy. There was nothing to keep Shangrin from taking the capital.

And take it he did, but that changed nothing. The dumbfounded barbarians entered the megalopolis of eighty-five million inhabitants, the only city on the most densely populated planet of the Empire. Suddenly awed by the huge buildings and the general grandeur of the city, they told the slaves they were free. Fires and shouts broke out here and there, with a colossal amount of looting. But the key Shangrin sought did not turn up. He decided to leave the megalopolis, perhaps because its great size reminded him too vividly of the peaceful cities of Neo-Sirius and Lorne. For a moment Gregory hoped that he might return on board the *Vasco*, but Shangrin did nothing of the sort. He went through a period of feverish activity, questioning all the scientists and scholars of the Empire who were brought to him as prisoners, all the pirate captains who came to him, lured by the hope of gain, all the arms-traffickers, pale weasel-faced individuals who came to beg for the right to loot the factories of the Empire. He spoke with members of the administration.

Following the Ulsar's lead, he placed his highest hopes in them. But all he saw were former slaves who had rebelled, war leaders, politicians. He got nothing from them that he had not already guessed. It was possible that they had been infiltrated by men as important as the Ulsar, agents of an unimaginable future, but he was unable to discover anything. Even the Runi was silent.

"You must help us continue the battle," Inoluno, one of the leaders of the rebel organization, said to him. "There's a lot more to be done. There are still a great many worlds which have not been liberated. The disorganization in space, where dozens of flags are floating, escapes description. There are worlds to be reorganized, new societies to be created."

"That is no concern of mine," Shangrin invariably replied. "I've told you what I want."

"Yes, I know," Inoluno would answer wearily, "but we've told you everything we could. You wanted to know who was supplying us with weapons, what power was helping us. We've told you. But there are so many worlds and empires between us and those hypothetical masters you want to reach, that we ourselves could never come face to face with them."

"Some of them have slipped into your ranks. Those are the ones I want. You think about it, for the sake of your future."

He could not be more explicit, nor Inoluno more sincere. Shangrin could not tell him that the Ulsar had

been the secret agent of an empire in an unimaginably
faraway time, which was why he had killed him. He
could not explain how he felt a mesh, like a spiderweb,
closing in on them. There was at least one agent per
planet, Shangrin believed, perhaps more, and they were
apparently linchpins of an organization secretly pursuing other goals. The sum total of what he could not tell
anyone, not even Gregory, kept growing. He sometimes
opened up with the Runi because the Runi was an alien
and he understood everything.

But all these interviews did provide Shangrin with a
better picture of the empires and the states surrounding
Xandra. Powers unknown to him until then sprang
out of the shadows and could be located on his charts.
Names took on meaning, substance. Horizons were
lighted up, peopled, animated. The population density
was incredibly thin but certain nations still maintained,
more or less consistently, contacts of varying degrees
of belligerency. Some traveled among the stars, others
did not, illustrating the different levels of technology.
Some of the neighbors of the defunct Empire were getting ready to nibble at its remains as if their under-
populated planets were not enough for them.

As Gregory put it, frogs and rats were becoming
active in the moats of the castle. This activity, laugh-
able or formidable, depending upon the point of view
of the observer, could well be the manifestation of a
battle waged on an inconceivably higher level. But the
manifestation remained inscrutable.

As time slipped by a vacuum formed around Shangrin. There was a change in the men who came to see
him. One day Inoluno disappeared; the deep upheavals
that shook the organization disposed of him—or was
there another explanation? Perhaps someone had been
afraid he would give Shangrin too much information.
The men Shangrin now saw were less open with him.
They hardly remembered what he had done. His questions were a nuisance.

Soon he felt cut off from the rebel organization. He
undertook operations on his own, on the basis of ques-

tionable information. He waged war, sold his fleet to
one power, then to another. He refused, whenever in-
vited to do so, to settle down, to establish his power.
He was, in a way, methodically putting into practice the
plan he had outlined to Gregory: he was shaking up
the world. He was stirring up the mud deposits in the
moats of the castle, hoping somewhere to destroy a
balance, arouse the anger of the gods until they came
face-to-face with him.

The three months went by. Gregory returned to the
Vasco and obtained another postponement. He stressed
the value of the loot Shangrin was piling up in the holds
of the great spherical ship and promised some sort of
settlement soon. They pretended to believe him, but
he could see Smirno's power growing; the hour of decision was drawing near.

"Why is he fighting a war?" Norma asked.

Gregory's fingers were playing with the young
woman's soft blond hair. He did not answer right away.
He wore on his face, like a mask, a grimace of sadness.
He gently patted Norma's shoulder before making up
his mind to speak.

"Because he does not want to give up his idea. He
swears it will get us back to our time."

"For a while I believed him," said Norma. "But now
I think he's mad. He's refusing to look squarely at
reality. He had a dream and he refuses to give it up."

"In his view, he is consistent," Gregory observed.

He himself no longer believed it. He pleaded Shangrin's case with the *Vasco* people out of loyalty, but
he pleaded the Magellanites' case with the captain, out
of honesty.

"Why do you keep going back to him? Sometimes
I wonder if you still love me."

It was an old, old question, one Gregory could not
answer. He could only look at Norma and stroke her
hair. He knew Smirno's influence on Norma was growing and that she was doing everything she could to
drive a wedge between him and the captain.

"He may be right," he said. "Since we're lost we might as well try everything. And even if he fails, our power will be so well established that we'll be able to live a long time in peace on the planet of our choice."

"Do you really believe that?"

"No," he said, turning away.

For there was a wake of fear in the hatred Shangrin had sown. The *Vasco* could withstand any storm, but for centuries its passengers and their progeny would be cursed in more worlds than could be seen in the sky of Xandra.

Then Shangrin scored a point and Gregory regained confidence. By checking and rechecking, the captain had discovered an artificial planet in the space between two stars. It was where pirate ships came to renew their supplies of all kinds of weapons. He captured it in a surprise raid and found only one man, who undertook to negotiate with him. The man claimed to be the representative of a distant empire, but Shangrin did not believe him. He knew he was in the presence of one of the players for the second time.

Shangrin lured him to his ship and brought him before the Runi. The man's expression changed suddenly.

"Traitor!" he cried. "You've made a deal with them."

His face grew ashen and he collapsed. Shangrin had taken no precautions against suicide, and he regretted it bitterly. The huge artificial planet exploded, destroying the crews Shangrin had left there to make a systematic inventory of its archives.

After this, Shangrin, accompanied by the Runi, asked himself some questions. Was this second player on the same side as the Ulsar? Or did he belong to the Ulsar's adversaries? In view of the political situation, this was the more likely possibility, for the artificial planet had furnished arms to the Empire, not to the rebel organization. But things were not so simple. A game of chess, even on a cosmic scale, would encompass sacrifices, gambits, strange reversals of strategy. Implicit in this game was the secret weakening of a point that was being overtly backed. The rules and the stakes of the game must be known facts before one could determine the psychology of all the players.

They found nothing unusual on the man—nothing but a metal cylinder, no thicker than a finger. Shangrin was absentmindedly turning it over and over in his hand, gauging with his fingers the sharp vibrations which stirred the atoms of the metal. The gesture became habit and he was hardly surprised when a precise, clear voice, speaking in his own tongue, issued from the bluish cylinder.

CHAPTER XII

The explosion of the artificial planet shattered not only the structures of space; it reverberated like a wave along the fibers of time. It finally reached the end of human history and the principal brain trying to co-ordinate the trillions of basal events that had occurred in a few hundred million years. It also shook the ulterior entities that governed time.

At first, there had been just the minor accident. But the disappearance from this sector of space of a depot of arms, even such a minor one, resulted first, in the loss of battles that ought to have been won; second, in the stillbirth of empires slated to come into being; and third, in the rise of others which, in the original game plan, had not been figured to emerge from limbo. These unfolded like fabulous flowers against the black screen of space.

The two antagonists—actually there were more than two, but they did not know it—saw their plans upset. The war, which had been fought openly on a front seven thousand years old and covertly in a jungle of several hundred million years, came to a halt. The drawback of tightly planned strategy was that it left no room for chance—unless it was of a purely problematical nature and consequently predictable within the framework of the laws of probability. The explosion of the artificial planet, together with other elements, was the grain of sand that clogged the machinery.

For a while.

Naturally the two antagonists had no illusions about the real origin of this accident, no more than they had about the real meaning of the war. But they knew the cause of the incident,—an entity named Varun Shan-grin—and what they needed to do to keep the disorder from spreading: either withdraw him from the game or move him from one square to another on the chess-board of time.

The high representatives of the antagonists, who were both human, at least in the sense of the word used at the extremes of history, met on neutral territory, in a subuniverse especially created for the negotiations in an absolute elsewhere. They were already acquainted with each other and must have dealt with similar situations in the past, which explained the relative cordiality of their conversation, even though each power, in theory, had vowed eternal hatred for the other.

"I have accepted this truce," said the Axelian representative, "because it is quite plain that the continuation of the present state of things can only harm us both equally. To be sure, the front has been moved, to your advantage, to several galactic groupings away, but you are quite aware of the instability of this advantage. There is the risk that a long series of vacillations will ensue. The economic principles which govern this ultimate war require that this absurd situation be ended."

The Nirvian representative paused a moment before reacting. They were exactly alike and each knew perfectly well what the other was thinking.

They could see, through the portholes which looked out on the real universe, the profusion of intermingling colored ribbons which represented matter writhing like snakes in the fluid discontinuity of time.

"Because of this Varun Shangrin we have lost an extremely able agent," said the Nirvian high commissioner. "You're the one who precipitated him into the distant past, therefore it's up to you to bear the brunt of the loss."

"Just a minute," said the Axelian. "We ourselves have lost an arsenal which was turning out to be of prime importance for our local offensive. At first it was nothing but a simple mishap. We never made the decision to send a ship of such primitive design back into a distant past. Our central brain simply neglected to correct this stupid accident at its inception because there was almost no likelihood of its degeneration."

"One cannot trust machinery," the Nirvian said between clenched teeth. "That is why we refuse to use an information mangle like your principal brain. Secondly, may I point out that you have endangered a ship which did not belong to any of the top belligerents and thus you violated the Charter of Conflict."

"We admit that," answered the Axelian. "We are therefore prepared to make reparation. We'll take this ship back into its space and time of origin. Of course, in order to do this, we shall be obliged to use fields of stasis on a large scale, which is also forbidden by the Charter."

"The use of these will be made under our direct control," the Nirvian interrupted. "But there is another aspect of the question that seems to escape you."

The Axelian, in his turn, paused. The colored ribbons in the unimaginable outside universe were reminiscent, in their mobile complexity, of a game of some sort, or a kaleidoscope destined for the amusement of a cosmic child. They represented, as they flickered, empires, trillions of beings, histories that were parallel as well as successive lives, dramas, struggles, suffering, solitude, stolen happiness, illusions and awakening consciences. At the level at which the two high commissioners sat, they could almost see the unrolling of the history of the universe and make sense out of it. But they knew that over them there were other entities playing with these colored ribbons and twisting them at will.

"The Runi," said the Axelian.

"Precisely," said the Nirvian envoy. "The main reason, the only reason we are in agreement, is the presence of the Runi aboard the *Vasco*."

"And our common hatred for the Runis is even greater than our mutual hatred."

"Just so," said the Nirvian.

They both thought exactly alike:

Every time they had a chance to destroy a Runi, they had to do so. If they could destroy them by becoming allies, they would become allies, but that was not possible. The Runis pulled the strings, which was why the humans hated them. They forced the humans to play this stupid, subtle, brutal game known as war, because they were gamesters; because the Runis had discovered that the most fascinating pawns were human beings; and because they manipulated human societies on the chessboard of the universe.

As soon as one game was finished, the two envoys acknowledged, another one began. Or perhaps there was only a single gigantic game, continually improved, repeated and transformed to the point of perfection. By this means, the Runis had led men to the limit of their capabilities and beyond; they had awakened in the human species capacities which were akin to dreams or mythology; they did not leave men in peace, and the humans experimented with things. Thanks to the Runis, the brief flames of human life had been imbued with suffering, conscience, loneliness and existence. But men hated them because the Runis forced them to tear each other apart.

It took mankind a long time to find out who called the shots. When they did, they realized that their consciences, as individuals, were of no avail: the Runis played the game according to the very rules of human societies. These rules were onerous and complex and could force men to act, in spite of their consciences, against their most secret or most fleeting wishes. The beings that the Runis moved on the chessboard of the stars were collective beings. Each man was nothing but an anonymous cell within these beings. Only a minority could try to withdraw from the game, but even then war caught up with it and forced it to defend itself or resign itself to destruction.

Only in the absolute elsewhere could men hope to escape the watchful eye of the Runis, because this was the edge of the chessboard. And that was one of the reasons why the high commissioners were meeting there, thinking such thoughts.

"He must be destroyed," said the Axelian.

"We cannot intervene directly," said the Nirvian.

"No. The Magellanites will give him up to us in exchange for return to their space and time."

"I hope so," said the Nirvian.

"Don't you think the Runis will intervene to save him?"

"I don't believe so. They never interfere in a game. For them it would probably be tantamount to cheating."

"I see that we are in agreement."

"Who is going to put the deal to them?"

"Let's draw for it," said the Axelian.

It fell to his lot. They were both silent for a long time, watching the ribbon game being played before them. A lavender fluorescence was winning out, then it burst and made way for a bluish fog whose convolutions for a moment seemed to dissolve the ribbons of light. The rules of this game were not intelligible to the men. Were they to become so, the end of the game would be near . . . but the Runis could manipulate and infinitely complicate these rules.

"One thing," said the Axelian. "I wonder what upheavals the disappearance of the Runi will carry in its wake. We have no way of estimating them."

"There is another worrisome point," said the Nirvian. "You have just seen the entire story of the *Vasco* and its captain unfold before your eyes. We can't find out at once what its outcome will be because that would force us to intervene in the temporal plan and the Charter forbids this. But remember its beginning. It was actually the *Vasco* which first made contact with the planet of the Runis."

"That's right," admitted the Axelian.

"And it is the *Vasco* captain, that Shangrin, who taught the Runis to play chess."

"I see what you mean," said the Axelian.

"But there's nothing we can do about it," sighed the Nirvian.

"It's too perfect a coincidence," insisted the Axelian. "It looks like a trick of the Runis."

"Stop speculating," said the Nirvian. "It will get us nowhere."

"Here is what we propose," said the clear, precise voice coming from the little bluish cylinder. "Your ship was hit quite unintentionally—a random shot which projected you into a period of time unfamiliar to you. You have caused so much trouble in the course of history that we are anxious to correct our mistake. We'll take you back to your time and space. It is impossible, for technical reasons, to take you across the time barrier as easily into the future as into the past, but we can place each of you in a field of stasis. This will permit each of you to cross painlessly two hundred and thirty million years. You will have to give up your ship and all your possessions, but you have our solemn promise that we shall replace them at your awakening; we will also watch over your safety during the two hundred and thirty million years of your sleep. We are prepared to indemnify you for the physical and mental hardships you underwent, in currency or in the metal of your choice.

"We make only one stipulation: you must give us the Runi you have on board and whom you are treating like an ally. You must realize that the Runi is a monster, that all Runis are monsters and, as such, are hateful and must be destroyed by the human species. In the distant future, from which we are speaking to you, two entities are engaged in a struggle to the death. You are feeling repercussions of this struggle, which is happening *for the sole amusement of the Runis*, to satisfy their monstrous appetite for games. In this distant future, which is to see the apogee of the human species, at the ultimate point of history, men have become pawns for the Runis to move at will on the chessboard of the stars.

"We are sure you won't hesitate for a second. We ask for no reparation for the agent you killed and the artificial planet you destroyed by forcing a high commissioner of the opposing team to commit suicide—the only course of action open to a man worthy of that name when in the presence of a Runi . . . death is preferable to submission. We only ask that you deliver the Runi to us."

"No!" shouted Shangrin.

Mingled fury and joy contorted his features. He threw the bluish cylinder on the ground, rushed up to Gregory and grabbed him by the shoulders.

"I've won," he shouted. "I've won! I've forced the gods to show themselves. The future belongs to us. I have unmasked the players."

"We are not the players," said the voice. "At least we are not the top players. Certainly we manipulate your societies and your destiny, but we ourselves are manipulated by the Runis. We know that, but in the present state of affairs, we can do nothing about it. The only real players are the Runis."

"Are you going to take them up on the deal?" asked Gregory hesitantly.

He saw in Shangrin's eyes the familiar piratical look and he knew the answer. Shangrin had shouted it out . . . he was not a man to go back on his word. He belonged to a world where the given word was as good as a written promise, where no one ever complained about a deal once it was completed, whatever the harshness of the preliminary discussions. A long time ago he had spoken of returning to their period of time in exchange for some rare and desirable products for the masters of time. But if he refused to pay the price they were asking, it was as if he had done nothing, as if the struggles had been in vain. Smirno would have every opportunity to turn Shangrin's final victory into defeat.

"No," said Shangrin.

And this refusal was aimed at Gregory as much as at the anonymous voice from the cylinder.

"Think," said Gregory. "It's our last chance. Our last chance."

"No," said Shangrin again.

The teapot was steaming before him in the control room of a primitive ship which had been captured on some astroport of the Empire. "I've entered into an alliance with the Runi. I told him we'd either get out with him or stay on with him. He came on board my ship of his own free will, and he is the guest of a Magellanite. A Magellanite has never betrayed his hospitality."

He looked up at a fragile goblet made of old porcelain. He placed it gently on the metal desk, looked at the alien stars shining on the navigation screen, and brought his fist down, smashing the goblet. All this was done almost noiselessly. He took the teapot in steady hands, removed the lid and sniffed the delicate aroma of the golden liquid. Then he threw the teapot into a corner of the tiny room.

"If I've succeeded," he said, "it's thanks to the Runi's help. Without him we'd still be sailing in darkness. If they want him, let them come and get him. They'll have the cannon of the Magellanics to deal with."

"But suppose they can prove what they say, that the Runi is a monster?" insisted Gregory.

"I know what the Runis are," said Shangrin. "I don't know what they will become in the future, but I know my Runi. He is not a monster. He doesn't cheat at chess."

"And what will the passengers of the *Vasco* say? Do you think they'll give up their return to the Magellanics that easily?"

"They will obey me," said Shangrin. And he got up and stretched to his full height. His hair and disheveled beard were now streaked with gray. He straightened up, firm and tall, all six feet six of his bear-like frame.

"You told me once that they wanted to colonize a virgin planet. I think it's a good idea."

His voice became softer, persuasive.

"I think it's a fine idea. I think I could sell it to them. And why should we believe what a metal cylinder says to us? Maybe we heard nothing. Maybe it was only an illusion."

"Then they'll never know you were right, Captain," said Gregory. "And I don't think that you'll be able to keep the truth from them. You cannot make a decision alone."

"There will be two of us to make it, Gregory," said Shangrin, "and you, at least, will know I'm right. Smirno, Henrik, Nardi, Derin, Zoltan, a bunch of technicians, their advice means nothing to me. It was in the name of everyone that I signed up."

His voice swelled and rumbled; it was like the tumult of great wild suns howling with the creaking of matter in voluted chambers.

"I accept the reparations for the damage done to us, but I do not accept the conditions. I shall continue the struggle. I'll bring those brazen masters of time to their knees. I'll make them roll in the dust."

The voice in the cylinder sounded thin and crackling after this thunderous outburst, but it was still clear and precise.

"There is no alternative to our bargain, Captain," it said. "If you refuse, we'll arrange to have your expedition wiped out by the very forces you unleashed. And you are not in a position to decide. We'll put the terms of our proposition, which we consider fair and just, to the crew of the *Vasco*; they will decide. We'll give you time to get back on board so that you can be the one to announce what we have decided in the names of Axelia and Nirv, who are invincible."

The cylinder gave out a brief green light, shattered and disintegrated.

The door opened noiselessly. It was too narrow to allow the Runi's egg to get through, so it was floating in the narrow corridor.

"It's your decision," said the Runi in his level voice. Then he left.

"Before you deliver the Runi you will have to wait

for us to have the necessary equipment in hand to destroy him," said the delegate from the future.

He was tall and slender. His eyes were cold, but strangely human as he addressed the council of the *Vasco*. He had told them who he was, that he had come from the ends of history, that after the passing of his civilization the fate of man was only a fog of tenuous probabilities, an inextricable entanglement of parallel realities. He told them he had assumed his present shape so as not to frighten them, and that, in any event, he was much closer to them than to the entities living on the other side of time who had sent him. He had suddenly appeared at the appointed hour in the council chamber. He might have been real or simply a projection.

They felt in him the reflection of an incomprehensible power and civilization. Even Gregory was fascinated by the envoy of the future, though he bitterly remembered the ovation that had greeted Shangrin when he had come back aboard, and the icy silence that had followed the announcement of his decision; he recalled the manner in which, in a split second, Shangrin had passed from the status of hero to that of a wild beast in their eyes. Gregory felt Norma's eyes on him, a heavy, suspicious look. He had come to hope that Shangrin had failed, that the Runi had been wrong in his original theories about the existence of the masters of time.

But the Runi and Shangrin, together, had been right. That, finally, was what the people on the *Vasco* held against them.

Gregory thought of the captain's request to make things drag along. He wondered now if he should obey him one last time, not because he was the captain but because he had always known what to do and what not to do. Gregory felt he owed him this delay even though he didn't know the reason for it.

He did not have any idea of what Shangrin was planning. And there was no one whose advice he could ask, not even Norma's, because he knew the answer would automatically be No. None of them had known Varun Shangrin as he had; they did not in the least feel bound by a madman's promise to a monster.

Gregory began to hate Norma with a violence that surprised him. He hated her because she no longer gave him the slightest support. He knew it would not last, but during that shattering moment he was alone, in spite of her, because of her. He was alone as Shangrin had been alone. When all was said and done he had become, willy-nilly, a reflection of Shangrin. It was Shangrin's decision he had to carry out.

CHAPTER XIII

"You have heard my proposition," said the envoy from the future.

The council had heard it . . . the council accepted it. All eyes turned to Shangrin's empty seat.

"I think this formality was necessary," the envoy of the future went on, "because your leader will not agree to deliver up the Runi. He apparently does not realize the monstrous aspect of that animal."

"He's an old man," said Smirno. "Recent events have deeply affected him."

He was staring insolently at Gregory. And so he had his revenge, Gregory thought as he consulted his watch. His hands were shaking, although he held them flat on the table. Shangrin had asked him to make the meeting last until the end of the fourteenth hour. He had agreed, but his heart was broken.

Three more minutes. He sought comfort in Norma's eyes, but a new hope gleamed in the young woman's gaze: her children would be born on Lorne, or Suni, and not in this hideous past full of wars and barbarians. To be sure, the millions of years' in the stasis field frightened her a little, but she would have gone through fire to get back to her own period in time . . . they all would.

What on earth could Shangrin be up to?

Two minutes.

"Let's move on to the vote," said Gregory.

"There's no point in doing that," objected Smirno. "Everyone agrees. The Runi will be delivered as soon as our friends from the future have the necessary equip-

ment at their disposal. I hope Varun Shangrin will have
no objection."

"*Captain* Varun Shangrin," Gregory protested.

"As you like."

Smirno turned toward the council.

"I propose that the text be amended to include the
dismissal of Captain Shangrin. His refusal to deliver the
Runi and his absence from our meeting betray only too
well his state of mind."

"He has the right to be heard," Gregory insisted,
even though he knew the game was lost. He hated
Smirno but he could not blame him. The Runi had to
be given up and, yes, Shangrin was mad—there was no
more room for doubt. And yet he had succeeded: he
had taken them where he had wanted, he had opened
the gates of time to them.

The results of the balloting were being written on the
board.

The hand on Gregory's watch passed the last second
of the fourteenth hour. He'd done what he could. So
be it. Let the Runi be given up and let us sink into that
sleep of two hundred million years. Only let it happen
quickly, he thought, before I go mad too.

Shangrin's voice yanked him out of his reverie. It
was powerful, crushing. It was the voice of the captain
of former days, the voice of the man who challenged
stars and time and the supreme magistrates of the Lesser
Magellanic Cloud. It was a voice ten years younger, the
voice of the bear, rolling like an ocean, cascading out
of the speakers like an avalanche.

What it was saying stunned them.

"I refuse the forfeit," said Shangrin. "As long as
I am alive, the Runi will not be given up. I refuse to
have him put to death. He came on board this ship of
his own free will and he is our guest. I would go down
to the depths of time rather than give up the Runi."

Gregory saw a strange smile forming on the lips of
the envoy of the future. What were the real sentiments
of the man who had come from the end of time?

"Shame on anyone who would think of giving up the

Runi," Shangrin went on. "He has done us no harm.
On the contrary, he has helped us as much as he could.
He cannot be held responsible for the threat that his
species may cause to hang over man. The Runi is my
ally and I will defend him."

Gregory looked around at the appalled faces of the
members of the council. Smirno was ashen. He was
listening, plainly frightened. Shangrin was only one
man and they had all ganged up against him, but they
had often given in to him before and something of the
habit remained.

"Since I can't be sure that all the members of the
crew wholeheartedly share my viewpoint," Shangrin
grumbled, "I have taken certain precautions. During the
two hours which have just elapsed, I have been locked
up in the control room, from which I can control the
ship's course. At the moment it is set for extra-galactic
space. In order to circumvent any attempt on my life, I
must warn everyone on board the *Vasco* that the generators' quarters and the navigation room have been cut
off from the rest of the ship. The flooding chambers
are closed and the partitions are in place. The corridors
and quarters near this sector of the ship must be
evacuated at once. Anyone found near here at the end
of the hour runs the risk of death."

"You're mad!" howled Smirno.

The words burst out. His mouth was twisted with
rage.

"Varun Shangrin, you are under arrest. You're fired.
You have no right to give orders on this ship anymore.
What you are doing is criminal."

Shangrin burst out laughing.

"Come and get me," he said.

"You've betrayed your fellow men. You've betrayed
the human species. You are a monster."

They all got up and started to shout. When he turned
around, Gregory saw why: space had just appeared on
the big screen. The ship was moving at fantastic speed
. . . the stars went by like fireflies gone mad. The ship

was going toward empty space—toward extra-galactic space—and already the stars were thinning out.

The envoy from the future waited for calm to be restored, then he looked at them coldly.

"It is not within my power to settle this affair," he said. "We are careful not to interfere in the affairs of primitive peoples when our interests are not at stake. It is up to you to handle this. I can only hope that these complications are only transitory. My offer still holds. In the present circumstances I see no reason for staying on board."

He disappeared suddenly. The Magellanites remained for a long time looking at the place where he had been, as if they could find a solution there. Gregory thought their fury had abated.

It had not, but their hopes had flown.

The robot-usher was going down the ship's corridors. From a secret drawer he had picked up, with his spidery metal fingers, a gold sword on a thin chain. He felt self-important but at the same time somewhat frightened. During two hundred and thirty-seven years of duty on various ships, he had carried the gold sword on its chain only three times, and each time it had meant the death of a man.

The robot was not afraid for himself, but his usual instructions forbade his harming a human. The little gold sword suspended this interdiction for a time and for a definite assignment, but the almost unconscious memory of all those years' interdictions weighed heavily on his limited, mechanical conscience.

He was going toward the center of the ship, carrying a heavy weapon that had been screwed like an eye into the center of his chest. Because of this he was only able to go in the main corridors of the *Vasco* as their thick partitions could withstand the destructive proximity of nuclear energy.

The humans along his path stepped aside and were silent. Nevertheless, the sensitive microphones of the robot-usher could pick up scattered words and fit them into the picture of the situation he was building up for himself.

". . . always considered the Runi to be a monster . . ."

". . . Major danger . . ."

"I cannot understand their allowing him on this ship where there are children."

"After all, those men from the future know what they are talking about, don't they?"

"Do you think that the *zotl* will slump, even taking into account our cargo . . ."

"That will depend upon . . ."

"To see Suni again . . ."

"I wonder if she waited for me . . ."

". . . Hibernation, obviously . . ."

Then there were fewer voices and, oddly enough, the robot-usher felt less worried. The hatred they bore the Runi made him uncomfortable. They hardly mentioned Shangrin; his turn would come later. Right now, they did not dare talk about him. It was to Shangrin the robot was to deliver the summons.

"Captain Varun Shangrin, Commandant of the *Vasco*, is ordered to present himself before the council to hear the terms of his dismissal and the decisions taken concerning the foreign monster known as the Runi."

When he reached the limit of the evacuated quarters, he ran into a patrol of explorers who stared at him coldly. They had remained loyal to Shangrin. The Magellanics meant less to them than to others. For the time being they were content merely to bare their teeth, but they would fight at a word from Shangrin. Their guardianship was ambiguous: they safeguarded Shangrin's mysterious plans and kept the *Vasco* passengers from venturing into the danger area.

The robot-usher wondered for a moment if they were going to shoot him, but the possibility that he himself might be destroyed did not really trouble him. The guards merely watched him proceed down the rectilinear passageway.

He could feel the torrent of energy coursing through the walls increase as he went forward. Sparks shot out

from the thin gold chain and the end of the small
sword. The discharge increased in intensity and framed
him in a dazzling light.

He had nothing to fear from obstacles of energy.
When he touched the first closed door a flame leaped
out and the paint on the door burned. The lock melted.
He tried unsuccessfully to work the latch then, carefully, with the help of his weapon, he cut a circular
opening in the door. He entered the generator room. It
was impossible to interrupt the generators without cutting off the energy supply for the entire ship, otherwise
he could easily have annihilated Shangrin and deacti-
vated the lethal walls.

He went through a second door and found himself
in a corridor that led to the spherical control room. The
now-rare stars on the huge curved screen danced crazily
by.

They followed the progress of the robot-usher on the
large screen of the council chamber. They saw him go
up to the control room in the center of the sphere. They
could see where Shangrin had linked up the various
computers so he could more or less control the ship's
progress. He was seated behind a bare table next to
which the Runi, in his egg, floated. The robot had
barely begun his speech, "Captain Varun Shangrin
. . ." when Shangrin's eyes took in the little sword. A
flash of anger broke out on his face and he took aim
with a heavy disintegrator. The robot-usher ought to
have reacted instantly, but he had caught sight of the
commandant's emblem on Shangrin's chest and had
hesitated.

A fatal error. The sword had not withstood the symbol of the power of the Magellanics; it melted, evap-
orated. The robot's armor resisted for a moment more
before yielding. In less than a thousandth of a second,
the superficial layers disintegrated, then the small
juridical conscience of the robot-usher expired. Its
ashes, the color of the void, fell forward on the screen,

toward an artificial abyss gaping amid the reflection of the stars.

"The guardians, the guardians," the council members shouted in chorus.

The noise was deafening. Gregory grew pale and ground his teeth. By destroying the robot-usher, Shangrin had put himself beyond the law. He had irredeemably violated the Constitution of Ships. He must have been mad. He could not hope to resist the guardians . . . no one could resist them—that was one of the things taught in the schools of the Magellanics. They could deal with mutineers, utterly destroy, if necessary, the ship that carried them. They were the ultimate guarantee of obedience to the law.

But they could not be called upon in just any circumstances. The innermost organization of the ship had to be in jeopardy. A special cybernator had been set up to evaluate the gravity of the threat and decide whether to use the guardians. Furthermore, in order to set off the cybernator, a two-thirds majority of the council members serving their term at that moment had to insert, each of them, a special key in his or her balloting machine.

Gregory noticed that Smirno, up on the platform, had also grown pale. He was gesturing, but his words were lost in the uproar. Gregory thought he was hesitating about unleashing the guardians. Actually, no one knew exactly what the guardians were. They could be machines of an infinitely more fearsome nature even than the robot-ushers or they could be *Vasco* passengers, mingling with the members of the crew, disguised as ordinary workers. Should the council so decide, power would be put entirely in their hands until the crisis had passed and law and order had been reestablished.

The robots emitted their strident whistle and calm was restored.

"I ask you to weigh carefully the decision you're going to make," Smirno said. "It is filled with consequences. Once the guardians have gone into action, it will be impossible to call them off until they have completed their task."

"We want the guardians," said a voice. Others echoed it.

"Very well," said Smirno.

His hesitation seemed incomprehensible, yet Gregory understood it.

Eighty-nine hands inserted eighty-nine keys into eighty-nine locks. Gregory's hands remained on his knees. He saw that Norma, having inserted her key, was looking at him. He did not stir. He could not betray Shangrin . . . not like this.

But the stars racing by on the upper screen were themselves a betrayal. What could Shangrin hope to achieve by that flight? What could the members of the council hope for from the guardians? The two questions complemented each other and canceled each other out.

"You asked for the guardians," said Smirno.

His voice was the voice of doom.

On the middle screen, which had become opalescent again after the destruction of the robot-usher, there appeared the sixteen stars of the central worlds of the Lesser Magellanic Cloud. It reawakened their homesickness. A deep voice came out of the speakers, at once familiar to them: the voice of someone who was not to be born for another two hundred and thirty million years and who was to become the president of the Navigators' Guild.

"Men and women of the Magellanics," said the voice, "you have called upon the guardians because a great crisis threatens you. During the sixty centuries of the history of our civilization only forty-seven thousand ships are said to have called upon the guardians. There probably have been others who never came back. I hope you will be luckier than they were.

"Men and women of the Magellanics, the guardians have taken many shapes in centuries past. I am perhaps the only one who has known them all, because this final recourse to the law must be adapted to the individual needs of each ship.

"I am going to tell you what the setup is for you. The master doors which cut off the various quarters of this ship are closed and only the chief guardian can unlock them. That leader is among you. He has been chosen on the strength of his experience and capabilities. Should he die during his tenure, he will be replaced by another who will remain nameless for the moment.

"Gregory, are you in this room?"

He got up, ashen, knees buckling. His answer was almost inaudible.

"Yes, I'm listening."

His reply had been unnecessary, for the robots were all staring at him. Their sensitive cells allowed the mechanical brain to observe him from its hiding place somewhere in the depths of the ship. It had remained inactive, blind, deaf, powerless until this moment. It was suddenly activated by the insertion of eighty-nine keys into their narrow openings. They had set off the voice of a man, not yet born, who was ordering everything in accordance with a law as yet unwritten. There was no possible escape.

"Good," said the voice. "You have been conditioned for the task you are going to undertake, but you did not know this. In their great wisdom, the chancellors of the Guild have decided to remedy human weaknesses as regards the law. Gregory, you are only the arm of the law and you will continue to be only this. That arm must be steady and strong; let no consideration of sympathy or interest stop you. That strength and that steadiness have been foreordained, and the knowledge of this law has been graven in your mind, as have many peculiarities of this ship, which will make of you the sole master of the situation. A hypnotic block has been set up in your subconscious which prevents you, at the present moment, from having access to this knowledge. It can be removed by a machine, several replicas of which are located in various places on board this ship. The robot-ushers will lead you to it."

"I refuse," said Gregory dully.

The mechanical brain, known informally as the

invisible chancellor, appeared to hesitate for a moment. In the precautions taken, Gregory recognized the attention to detail typical of the commercial sharpness of the distrustful rulers of the Lesser Magellanics, and he felt a mounting nausea at the thought of the labyrinth into which he was being propelled.

"You have no choice, Gregory," said the voice.

The chancellor must have chosen from among the various possible registers the tones of the man who was not yet born. Deep down in its metal entrails all sorts of answers must be lying dormant, ready for every possible question.

"You have no choice. The robot-ushers are henceforth detailed to force you, if necessary after twelve hours, to undergo the treatment which will free you from hypnotic suggestion.

"Don't be afraid, Gregory. As soon as your mission has been accomplished you will be given back to yourself, you won't remember anything of what has happened. You must rise above yourself, above your personal preferences and become, for a time, the embodiment of Magellanic justice.

"To assist you, you will have the robot-ushers with gold swords. Any men you choose will undergo psychological training. No one can refuse what you ask.

"Your adversary, whoever he may be, will not be able to escape your justice. This is the law and it must be carried out.

"If something happens to you, someone else will take your place. Done under my seal, I, Arno de Lurve, Archon of Suni and Lorne, merchant prince of the Lesser Magellanic Cloud and Chairman of the Navigators' Guild."

The voice was still.

"I can't do it," said Gregory.

But he could scarcely be heard. The robot-ushers bowed to him and formed an honor guard around him. He felt a hand groping for his; he turned and saw Norma's blond hair, her clear blue eyes and bloodless lips.

"You must," she whispered. "You must."

He pushed her aside and cleared a passage to the exit; the robots followed him. Questioning looks turned toward him. He straightened up and forced himself to walk slowly, realizing that there was no escape; the robots would stick close to him and guard him against any possible mishap, against his will, if need be.

He had twelve hours left.

A man got up and beckoned to him. It was Arno Linz, the boatswain, Shangrin's old companion, the toughest man on board.

"Gregory, you're not going to let them put this over on you. Nothing is lost yet. My men are holding the center of the ship and they won't let—"

"Arno Linz, you are under arrest," said a robot-usher.

"Come and get me," retorted the warrant officer, pulling a weapon from his pocket.

A blinding ray struck him between the eyes. He collapsed, his body falling like a puppet against the back of a chair. A small dark spot over the bridge of his nose began to bleed.

This was the first bloodshed . . . there would be more. Each robot-usher had a small gold sword.

CHAPTER XIV

The news was alaarming. The Exploration sector had just announced that no one would be allowed near the control room except by order of Shangrin himself. His men were ready to open fire. They would not give way to the guardians.

"Civil war?" asked Norma, looking up questioningly at Smirno.

"I'm afraid so," said Smirno. "They have heavy weapons at their disposal. They can resist for a long time unless Gregory is willing to give in and then, somehow, manages to make them see reason.

"Meanwhile, we are getting further and further away."

"I don't want anything to happen . . ." said Norma in a voice which suddenly broke.

She started to cry and turned toward the wall as sobs shook her.

"Stop it," said Smirno.

He wanted to appear tough but he only succeeded in being disagreeable. He himself felt shaken by what had just happened.

Henrik came into Smirno's office.

"Listen," he said, "something must be done. Gregory must be forced to accept, at once. Not in twelve hours. We are moving away at full speed from the stellar cumulus of Xandra, and as most of Navigation's computers are disconnected, we'll never find our way again. We are lost."

Doubly lost, thought Smirno. Lost in time and space. Lost between irresolution and revolt, between loyalty and the law.

"I have tried to get in touch with Shangrin," he said. "He refuses to listen to me. He says he will turn the ship about when we have changed our minds."

"Who is that?" asked Henrik, pointing to Norma.

Smirno shrugged.

"Norma Shundi, Gregory's fiancée, or something of the sort."

Henrik's bald pate quivered. His eyes grew round.

"If anyone can sway him, she must be the one. Why haven't you sent her?"

"She refuses. She is afraid for him."

"Is everyone here afraid?"

"Aren't you afraid?"

"I, I . . ."

"Well then, keep quiet."

The Runi must love this, Smirno said to himself. What a complex game this was, with chessmen moving in every direction. He went up to Norma and put his hands on her shoulders. He hated himself for what he was about to tell her.

"You're going to find Gregory," he said dully. "You're going to convince him he must undergo the treatment. Otherwise he will die. Otherwise, in less than twelve hours, the robots will kill him, and someone else will be chosen."

She turned slowly and stared at him as large tears welled up. He said to himself that she must have seen through his lie, but he read on her lips, in her mute cry, that she believed him. He looked away.

Supposing it's true, he thought. Supposing I am on the list. If I was next in line, what would I do, what would be my reactions? An icy shiver ran up his spine. Would I accept, unhesitatingly, the operation that would turn me for a few hours, for a few days or for eternity, into an infallible engine of destruction, the ultimate incarnation of Nemesis?

It could happen to me.

The thought of his possible sacrifice went through him like a burst of fresh air, like a promise of peace.

He could take Gregory's place, he thought, and all would be well. Perhaps he would survive and, for once, he would have been Smirno, the chosen man, the man of action. But it wasn't possible. It was unlikely that he was on the list—he had probably never been properly conditioned. And the invisible chancellor would probably not let him take Gregory's place. Each one had to fulfill his own destiny. A man is replaceable only when he must be replaced, because he has disappeared.

"Go find him," he said.

He spoke through clenched teeth.

"Yes," she said at last.

He looked up and saw in her eyes a determination so ruthless that even Shangrin might have paused.

"I don't want to see anyone," said Gregory into the speaker.

"Not even me?" she asked.

"Not even you."

"You don't love me anymore?"

Pause.

"I don't know."

Then: "This is hardly the time."

She forced herself to say very quickly; "Gregory, you can't wait there. Gregory, you don't want our children to live in this horrible past. Oh, Gregory, you don't want me never to see Suni and Lorne again, the gardens of Lorne where I met you? Gregory, you can't hesitate. On one side there is only an old man and a . . . a foreigner. You can't weigh them against thousands of children, women, men. Gregory, you have no right to do so! You're like Shangrin. You are now his successor and he has never let his people down. He has always come to their rescue. You must do as he has always done . . . you must save them, even against him."

He did not answer. She stared hard at the screen and tried to read in his face that he had heard her, but he seemed deaf. His eyes were unblinking. Only his upper lip trembled imperceptibly where minute drops of sweat were gathering.

"Gregory," she said.

He saw the woman's lips flatten against the screen, her features distorted, then her hair brushed against the screen as though she were trying to reach him physically through that technological thickness.

He turned off the switch. The screen grew dark.

He had to speak to Shangrin; he had to get to him before he turned into a machine. He felt that he could at least put as much energy into speaking with Shangrin as he would use up later in trying to bring him around. He turned and saw the robot-ushers: a black swarm, outlined by the sign of the slender sword.

He had to escape them first.

The great ship plowed into the void or, more precisely, into Second Space. Shangrin's alterations in his navigational system had dangerously weakened the margins of safety of his course. He was brushing against chronic aberrations in subspace that could wipe them all out of the continuum without so much as a bang.

"They're complaining that you're doing nothing," Henrik was saying to Smirno. "They are beginning to form combat groups. They've raided an arsenal and found isolating contraptions; they're breaking through main doors. They say they will wipe out the explorers, get to the navigation sphere and capture Shangrin."

"Who is their leader?" asked Smirno. "What are the robot-ushers doing?"

"I don't know who their leader is. It's rather an anarchic movement. There are several gangs operating separately and they'll attack anybody, including the robots. The robots, in the absence of orders to the contrary, don't dare use lethal weapons, so they are being destroyed one by one."

"Who could stop them?"

"I don't know. I tried—I didn't succeed. Gregory, perhaps.

You ought to try."

"You think like I do, don't you?"

"They're going to get themselves massacred."

"Yes. They don't know how to fight. The men in the Exploration Sector do. Only Shangrin can stop the mess."

Henrik stroked his bald pate.

"He can't be reached. He doesn't answer anymore."

"I'm going to try to speak to them."

Smirno juggled with the switches of the communicators. He tried to clear his throat but couldn't relax the lump that paralyzed his vocal cords.

"Stop and listen to me," he said in a voice squeaky with emotion. "I am talking to you, men of the Exploration Sector who want to defend, over and beyond the call of duty, a man who has condemned you to a fate without issue. I am also addressing those who have seized weapons illegally, in a desperate, disorganized, futile and murderous attempt. The situation is bad enough without adding . . ."

His voice trailed off and broke. Like an undertow, like a long murmur of the sea, he could hear from all over the ship the boos that greeted his speech: hatred, terror, violence in their purest state.

He consulted his watch. He had ten hours left. He still had half the ship to cross, the gangs of armed mutineers to avoid, the barrages of the exploration crews to surmount and death lurking in the walls to escape.

He undressed, took out of a closet a well-insulated spacesuit and put it on. He hesitated a second, then picked up a weapon. The robot-ushers watched him without making a move. They would intervene only if he turned it against them.

He grabbed a phone and dialed a number.

"Smirno?" he said. "Can you hear me?"

"I hear you," said Smirno.

"All right. I am going to try to get in touch with Shangrin, make him change his mind. Is there some way of talking to him? I couldn't do it on the normal circuits."

"Neither could I. He must have short-circuited the wires."

"Well then, I am going to go there," said Gregory. "I'm going to try to get through."

"Why don't you accept the treatment?"

"Because," said Gregory.

"Well, I see your point in a way. What can I do to help you?"

"Do you know how to reach the control sphere?"

Silence.

"Henrik says that you can try Simili Park Number three, and go from there by the canal system in the bottom of the lake. You will reach the cooling circuit of the generators. If you manage to make an opening in the right place, you'll come out right next to the sphere."

"And the lake will empty into the generators?"

"No. The breach will be closed instantly. But there is radiation. You have one chance in a thousand to get out."

"I'm going to risk it," said Gregory. "One more thing. How can I get rid of the ushers?"

"I don't see how," Smirno admitted.

"All right. I'll find a way, otherwise they won't let me go on to the end."

Smirno hesitated.

"I . . . I wish you luck, Gregory."

The door opened in front of him. He glanced down the corridor. It was empty. He went slowly up to the great radial artery of the ship. He could see, at the end of the tube, silhouettes darting between cold flashes of light.

He turned his back to them. He hurried along and went off diagonally into one of the secondary corridors. He was looking for a well that would lead him to Simili Park. He carefully examined each doorframe before going on. He kept turning around.

He came without difficulty to a well. His heart was pounding as he unlocked the well and contemplated the cylindrical shining depth stretching below him. Wells were not normally used for moving from one place to another in the ship, but they did connect the different levels and, in an emergency, allowed passage from one to the other in a minimum of time.

He jumped. The degravitational field slowed his fall. The wall was so perfectly smooth and even that it was difficult to see if he was actually moving.

When he heard voices rising from the bottom of the well he realized he had made a mistake—he was landing in the middle of a group.

He saw at a glance that it was a gang of mutineers. Their weapons were varied and they semed to be without a leader. He had taken them by surprise, but he didn't stand a chance of escaping them, and he had no time to waste in explanations.

He lunged into the only empty space. A hand grabbed his shoulder and, pushed off-balance, he pivoted. That saved him, for a beam went by his head. He rolled up into a ball and tried for the shelter of a wall. Simili Park was a few steps away but he had to cross open terrain to get to it. He heard the others shouting questions and orders. He had been recognized—they were after his blood. The mutineers seemed to think that if he was killed, his successor would have less hesitation in submitting to the treatment, which would solve the crisis more rapidly.

He slipped his weapon from its sheath, aimed carefully and pulled the trigger. The radiant beam cut through the metal of the ceiling, which collapsed in a cloud of sparks. Live cables short-circuited and fire began to spread. The sprinkling system went into action instantly in the thick smoke. He leaped from his shelter and rushed toward the park.

The smoke made him choke. He fought his way through a welter of shapes that must have been the men looking for him, so close he could have touched them. He took advantage of their confusion to reach Simili Park.

It consisted of a landscape of sand and dunes, set

up only the night before. Wide palm trees shed clear shadows under a torrid sun.

Men leaped out from groves of trees. They did not shoot immediately as they tried to figure out from whom he was escaping and to what side he belonged. Then his pursuers shouted something and the new arrivals tried to cut him off; he had been identified.

A spotlight picked him up just as he was going over the crest of the dunes sloping down steeply toward the lake. He rolled into a ball and tumbled down the length of the slope. A sharp pain shot through his ankle when he tried to get up. He saw along the top of the wall of sand his pursuers taking careful aim at him. He closed his eyes.

But death did not come. He heard shouts, but no finger of fire touched him. He sat up in the sand and started to rub his sprained ankle, then he looked up. He owed his safety to the robots who had followed him. They scattered the assailants before floating down toward him slowly and majestically.

This time they would not let him go. He got up as quickly as he could and took a few steps toward the lake. The water was soon up to his thighs; he plunged in and started to swim.

The robot-ushers flew directly over him, plainly wondering how they were going to fish him out. He dived under to get away from them, trying desperately, under the lukewarm water, to adjust the breathing apparatus of his suit, but he didn't succeed at first and had to surface. He took a deep breath and saw the robots, like giant june bugs, dive-bombing him.

He plunged again and finally succeeded in adjusting the respirator. Then he swam with powerful, rhythmic strokes toward the bottom. He had to make a tremendous effort to remain on the bottom because he was insufficiently weighted.

A long black shape sped before him. It took him a moment to recognize it as one of the robots. They had not given up their idea of saving him; they could not, in fact, abandon him.

He was trying to follow the channels in the bottom of the lake. He finally saw in the clear water the large apertures, surrounded by small whirlpools, of the water intakes. They were covered with grids.

The robot-ushers stayed as close to him as a school of sharks. He struggled with the grate locks but, unable to open them, shot them out. The grids gave way in a maelstrom of vapor. He hid in the protective darkness of the channels, which were just wide enough for him to go forward. There, at least, the robots would be unable to follow him.

He let himself be carried by the current. The lake water was used to cool certain parts of the generators, but it was divided up among a great number of reservoirs and he had to keep from getting lost in that labyrinth.

At the first branching off, he placed his ear against the wall and tried to detect a vibration. He chose the direction from which the most noise came and groped his way about for some time in the total darkness of the ship's entrails like a monstrous fish lost in a cavern.

He finally realized where he was. Those enormous parallel tubes, he was sure, went through the generator room. But which wall should he cut through? Some of the tubes were dozens of yards above the ground. Others went right through the core of the generator. He had to keep as close as possible to the bottom and as far as possible from any sources of radioactivity. He tried to reconstruct mentally the plan of the labyrinth.

He finally grappled with the canal wall at a bend. It resisted for a time, then gave way all at once. He was pushed through by the rushing torrent and thrown to the bottom, barely a yard lower down. He remained stunned on the metal floor, which was already being dried up by pumps. A siren went off.

He pulled himself up on his forearms and smiled wryly. He had accomplished the first part of the operation. He consulted his watch: less than an hour had passed since he had told Smirno his plans. Action-time was also relative.

The hardest part, if not the most time-consuming, still remained to be done—reaching Shangrin and, above all, persuading him.

CHAPTER XV

"Get up!" the guard shouted.

Dazed, Gregory stared at him. The guard had a tough face and a shaved head. He was wearing a complete explorer's outfit and handled his weapon as easily as a tool. He came up to Gregory and, seeing that he was not moving, kicked him.

"Who are you?" he asked. "Where did you come from?"

Gregory painfully tore off his respirator.

"Gregory," he said, "I've come to speak to Shangrin,"

He knew the guard. He feverishly groped for his name but memory failed him.

"Gregory," said the guard. "You've gone over on the other side. You had Linz killed, huh? And you're after the old man now. Well, you're out of luck."

He slowly raised his weapon. Gregory gestured frantically.

"Stop. Don't be silly. I've come to try to save him. Can you take me to him?"

The guard hesitated. Gregory remembered him as part of the expedition on Xandra, at that time under Gregory's own command. The other could not have forgotten.

"Do you really think I would betray him?" he asked.

"Don't move," said the guard. "I may be making a mistake, but I'll give you one chance."

He whistled. Several men came up, one of whom was a junior officer.

"You're crazy," said Gregory, getting up as they pointed their weapons. "You are under my orders. I'm second in command on board this ship."

"I follow only Shangrin's orders," said the officer.

But Gregory noticed that he was weakening. Old disciplinary reflexes were still functioning.

"Shangrin won't approve . . ."

"He asked us to stay here," said the explorer. "He gave orders to let no one through, neither man nor machine."

"Tell him I'm here."

Gregory spoke clearly and with authority. His sprained ankle hurt so badly he could hardly stand up, so he leaned against the wall. He saw panic in the officer's eyes.

"We're no longer in touch with him—he's disconnected all the intercoms. He said he wanted peace and quiet."

Gregory shook himself. Water dripped from his clothing.

"I *must* speak to him."

"Have you undergone treat . . . treatment?" the leader asked hesitantly.

"Do you think I'd be in this state if I had?" Gregory burst out. "Do something and do it fast! You'll be under attack any minute now."

"We're not afraid of anyone."

They were rocks of stubbornness.

"Do you really want to shoot Magellanites, kill Magellanites?"

They looked at one another. After a pause the officer made up his mind.

"Get rid of your weapon and come forward."

"Tell one of your men to help me. I can't walk."

They looked at one another for a moment, then the leader nodded. One of the men put down his weapon and came up. Gregory leaned on his shoulder and walked, wincing.

"Anyway, it won't do any good," said the explorer. "We can't communicate with the captain."

"He's still in the control room?"

"He's retreated to the room behind the computers."

"Can I get within shouting distance?"

"Maybe. We didn't try."

"Let's go," said Gregory.

They were a strange procession as they went through the huge generator room.

"There is current running through all the walls of the control room, so don't touch anything."

"Thank you," said Gregory.

He went ahead, with the assistance of the guard, up to the circular door of the celestial sphere. He could see the navigation dome at the end of the narrow gangplank which looked as though it were suspended above a void. Beyond it was the opening of the corridor and, at the end, the cubicle where the computers reflected in silence on the ship's course. Shangrin had taken refuge with the Runi. A real rat hole.

"Shangrin?" he called.

His voice reverberated in the sphere as though it had been reflected by the stars, repercussed by the invisible vaults of that fleeing universe. He filled his lungs.

"Shangrin!"

Then he listened. He thought he could perceive, beyond the narrow rectangle of light from the door, a rustling, as if a heavy mass were being dragged along the floor. He took a step forward.

"Look out!" said the guard, but Gregory paid no attention to him.

"Shangrin!" he shouted. "It's me, Gregory."

Shangrin's voice finally reached him, magnified by a megaphone. It exploded in that restricted space.

"Go away," Shangrin was saying. "Go back to your friends."

Gregory waited for the echo to die down.

"Come back, Shangrin, come back. The ship is a mess. You're surely not going to let your men kill each other. Come back, Shangrin, it's not too late."

He waited for silence. His words had to go across a sphere—a microcosm of the universe—and reach the little gods who had taken refuge on the other side of the ersatz sky, in a metal cave. All around them, in the rest of the ship, chaos had been rampant since their

withdrawal. This was probably Shangrin's view of the
situation from where he sat, deep in the heart of the
ship, as it raced through the real universe at a speed
steadily increasing in time.

"It's no good, Gregory," said Shangrin. "I've made
up my mind."

"But you have no way out."

He lowered his voice.

"Can the Runi hear me?"

Dead silence.

"Yes," Shangrin finally answered. "He's right next to
me."

"I'd like to speak with you alone."

"Can't be done. I'll never come out."

"Very well," said Gregory. "Let the Runi hear what
I have to say."

He cleared his throat. His voice was already hoarse
from shouting. . . . Maybe he was shouting uncon-
sciously because he wanted to be heard everywhere.

"You can't really sacrifice the *Vasco*, the men and
women entrusted to you, to a foreigner, to an alien.
Come back. There's still time to straighten everything
out. They'll carry you in triumph."

"No," said Shangrin. "Leave me alone. I'm too old,
it's your turn now."

"Then let me come in. Let me take the *Vasco* back
to its point of departure. You're losing us."

Shangrin roared in fury—but it was a weary roar.

"Do you think I'm mad too? All I ask is time! I'm
going to straighten this out. Don't you suppose I've
asked myself all those questions?"

"Well then, what are you waiting for? What are you
doing?"

The answer was slow in coming.

"I've made a deal with the Runi," Shangrin said
slowly. "I'm playing chess. I proposed one last game.
If I win, he will settle for his life; he'll run away at
once and try his luck in space. If I lose, I shall have
to do what I promised. I need time . . . I must win.

Let me be, Gregory, tell the others to give me a few hours."

Gregory's shoulders slumped.

"He is mad," he said softly, to himself.

The guard heard him and looked at him, an unfriendly gleam in his eye.

Gregory made one last effort to reason with Shangrin.

"But if you win, you will have nothing more to sell to the masters of time. You won't get your people back to their era like you promised you would."

"I'll never see the Magellanics again, Gregory. I know that. But my people will, unless I lose. But I won't lose . . . I am taking drugs to stimulate my mind. The Runi was willing, he accepted the handicap. Go back to your friends."

"It's a fascinating game," said the Runi, his voice crystal clear.

"But why, why?" shouted Gregory.

"I have entered into an alliance with another people, Gregory. I shall fulfill my obligations, that's all. Is there a guard with you?"

"Yes."

"Well then, he must take you back to the council. I forbid you to stay in this part of the ship."

The rectangle of light on the other side of the ship shrank and the door slammed.

"Come on," said the guard.

Gregory leaned on him and, filled with despair, left to find the exploration crews. The officer came up to him, sneering.

"The robot-ushers came as far as here," he said. "All they want is to take you away."

As Gregory looked at the robots he realized there was a distant kinship between them and the Runi's egg: they represented the same inhuman, impenetrable side of the universe. They picked him up very gently as he closed his eyes and allowed himself to be carried through the deserted corridors.

Gentle hands slid along his body, absorbing the pain. He was lying down, eyes closed, thinking. Voices floated over him. They seemed to be raised in an incomprehensible prayer.

He was thinking about the game being played in the center of the ship between the captain and a demon; its only point seemed to be the concern of an old man for his own personal ethics. Or was there something deeper which Gregory couldn't put his finger on, but which he vaguely felt? The game could be the means of communication between two species; it had to be played to prevent a definitive misunderstanding between them. The consequences of the game could spread like waves in the fluid substance of time, along the series of moves alternately played by unimaginable players. The game, for Shangrin, could be the ultimate means of throwing light on the innermost nature of the Runi, and for the latter, the best method of gauging human nature in its infinite variety. Passion as well as reason presided at the game . . . the whole future face of history could depend upon this confrontation. There was a striking parallelism between the game being played by Shangrin and the Runi, and the infinitely greater one being played by the Runis who, according to the envoy of the future, were moving humans, like so many pawns, on the chessboard of the stars.

He clearly saw the stars form into a chessboard, then the board spun quickly and collapsed in the middle, and he fell into a well of gold and night as the whispers around him grew more audible.

He came slowly out of a deep sleep. He blinked and recognized Smirno, Norma and Zoltan looking down at him anxiously.

"I don't want the treatment," he said.

It was an obsession. He turned it over in his mind, then gave it up. A sort of curtain was torn inside him. He suddenly felt more mature and surer than he ever had before. He understood more clearly the *Vasco's* situation and he knew what he had to do. It was absolutely essential that Shangrin be protected, against his will, if necessary. He also knew more about the workings of the ship than he ever had before. He suddenly remembered the secret passages whose existence he had completely forgotten, and switches that could either cut or supply energy to the different parts of the ship.

"It's too late," said a cold and distant voice which he recognized as Smirno's. "You have just had the treatment. Successfully. How do you feel?"

"Well," he said indifferently.

He examined, logically, all the possibilities. He did not in the least feel inhuman; he did not hate Shangrin nor anyone else. On the contrary, it seemed to him he understood Shangrin better and respected him more than ever. The mist in his mind shrouding his thoughts about Shangrin's actions had been dispelled. All the little secondary emotions which had hampered the exercise of his intelligence and sensitivity appeared clear to him, unimportant now. He realized that Shangrin was neither a god nor a hero, but a man, like him, and what he had done he had chosen to do, as a man.

I see, he said to himself.

He got up effortlessly and looked curiously at the instruments surrounding him. They were simple: a minute marble, glistening with light, revolving and jumping in a magnetic field. The eye could hardly follow it. It oscillated to rhythms engraved in the mind.

"I'll need thirty men," he said. "Volunteers only. All the others must surrender their weapons. I suppose they'll obey me now."

"Not the exploration crew, I'm afraid," said Smirno. "But are you sure you don't want to rest before starting?"

"He looks in first rate condition to me," said Zoltan, the biologist.

"I want the men to be ready in half an hour," Gregory said.

He tried his leg. It felt a bit weak still, but the pain had gone. He could walk unaided.

Then he had an idea. "How long have I been sleeping?" he asked.

"About seven hours," Zoltan said. "You didn't say anything in your sleep. All we know is that you got in touch with Shangrin. What is he doing?"

Gregory hesitated imperceptibly. Seven hours. The game must have proceeded in all its complexities; it might even be over. He could not tell them about the game. . . . They would not understand.

"Nothing," he said. "He is waiting."

There were thirty-one of them, threading their way through the secret passages of the ship toward the central navigation sphere. Gregory was first. He was now familiar with a maze of wells, canals and manholes secretly built into the ship by the distrustful builders. They reached the cables which provided Shangrin the current to isolate his section of the *Vasco*. They disconnected them and, in the sudden darkness, went forward by the beam of headlights, like strange glowworms headed for the conquest of an enormous artificial fruit.

They reached the generator room. Gregory's voice burst out, reverberated in darkness filled with expectation and hatred.

"Surrender," he said to the exploration crew. "You can't get away."

Beyond them, he was speaking to Shangrin. He hoped he was listening, that he would answer, give the necessary orders. But he heard nothing except oaths and challenges. Then he gave a signal and a light, odorless gas issued from thin capsules. The volunteers waited for a few moments in silence in the dark, then they heard the thuds, occasionally muffled by distance, of falling bodies. The explorers had not had the time to take in what was happening to them and put on their masks. They were all fast asleep.

"Stay here," Gregory said to his men.

He groped his way forward, alone in the dark, not daring to light his torch and show himself as a target for any guard who might have escaped the gas. He glided slowly to the door of the sphere, knowing that he was silhouetted against the stellar horizon. He waited. The shot he expected did not come. Then he called again in his radiophone.

"Shangrin? Shangrin? Listen to me."

The stars fled, disguised as slender rays of light. He felt utterly alone.

"I've come back, Shangrin."

Silence. A nameless anxiety gripped him. He tried to imagine what had taken place between the old man and the Runi. The Runi could not make his escape from the center of the ship.

"Shangrin!"

The door at the end of the gangplank remained obstinately closed, a deadly current still flowing through it. He couldn't neutralize the power without at the same time cutting off the energy source of the cybernators, which would have caused instant disaster to the entire ship.

'Shangrin?" he called.

He took a step forward. He heard a sort of rustling in the silence.

"Wait," said a voice. "Wait, give me another minute."

He did not recognize it at first, but it could only be Shangrin's voice. It was weak and worn out, as old as if it had come from a toothless mouth. It was redolent with the weariness of a million years spent traveling through worlds.

Gregory knew what worries had haunted it, what drugs . . . drugs which stimulated the brain but exhausted the nervous system, lowered the reaction time but wore out nervous cells, consuming their medullary sheaths . . . drugs which made a mind work a thousand times faster than normal and then shriveled it up.

"Shangrin?" he shouted.

"Give me a few more minutes," the voice whispered. "I . . . I'm almost through."

"Check," said the Runi.

Gregory stiffened. The nape of his neck grew icy.

He wanted to call out again, but it was senseless now. It would be just as senseless to hurl himself against the lethal door, to cross the bridge over the stars. He strained to listen. He heard something like a gurgle and he thought he heard the sliding of wooden pieces on a chessboard, but it was only an illusion, perhaps only the song of those imaginary stars following their unimaginable trajectories.

"Checkmate," said Shangrin.

And in the sound of that word there was something of Shangrin's former overbearing attitude, his biting irony, his arrogance, a shadow of his former haughtiness.

"Shangrin?" called Gregory.

"Just a few more seconds, just a few," the voice implored.

Metallic noises emanated from the silence, the sound of springs being broken or stretched. He said he'd liberate the Runi here and now, Gregory thought, but how? Did he want to clear a passage to the inside, to one of the launches of the _Vasco_, embark the Runi on it and let him loose in outer space? He wondered what his men, left behind in the dark, were thinking. He had come alone, not to accept the decision of the gods but to force them to give in, and here he was waiting. He was the only one who knew what he was waiting for, and he would remain the only one.

Gregory told himself that he could still risk everything, rely on his insulated outfit, force open the door, keep the Runi from . . .

He went forward on the narrow gangplank almost up to the door and started counting. He could afford to give these moments to Shangrin. He could take it upon himself to grant them to him, because they were no longer of any importance. If Shangrin took too long, he would not hesitate any more.

"You may come in now," said Shangrin's voice, faraway, weary, weak.

CHAPTER XVI

Gregory put his hands on the door, half-expecting a deadly shock to put an end to his life, shrivel him in a flash, not even giving him time to scream. It didn't come, the door was inert. The torrent of energy had been stopped. He pushed harder until the door gave. He went through the dark control room, then through the corridor, forcing himself to walk despite a sudden and frightening exhaustion. The light bulbs had burned out when the walls had been electrified. The light he had seen the first time came from the corner where Shangrin had retired. It was strange to go forward, groping one's way, through the familiar corridor; it was like rediscovering it as one's feet and hands parted the darkness and brushed against the partitions on either side.

A door at the end of a corridor. He shoved it with his foot and it pivoted. The first thing he saw in the blinding light was the Runi's egg. Empty. Spread all around it was a profusion of wire, the whole tight and complex network which had imprisoned the Runi and allowed him to talk like a man.

That reminded him of something. He remained still for a moment, trying to keep his balance and struggling with his memory to dig up a recollection. Then it came to him: that gold and silver complex, those subtle feelers, looked altogether too much like a lie detector. Why hadn't he thought of it sooner? The Runi's translation system worked exactly like a lie detector. And the Runi must have known it.

This threw a worrisome light on certain events. He made an enormous effort and again searched his memory; he remembered circumstances when the translating system had seemed out of whack, when the machine had stammered.

He saw, in a flash, that the Runi had been lying, that he had forced the machine to disguise his thoughts. Gregory tried but he hadn't the strength to recall those occasions. It was of no avail anyway, since the Runi had gone, but perhaps he had lied from the very beginning. Perhaps he had always played a part, a solitary game, carefully, diabolically. And now he had fled. Even the secret of his flight belonged to him, possibly a way of vanishing in the imaginary space of fictitious stars. Or he might have known the secret which allowed the envoy of the future to appear or disappear in a flash. It did no good to speculate, since there was no one now who could answer. The Runi would probably never find his own people again, nor return to his own period in time.

Gregory shook his head. He wanted to laugh, a weary, sad, bitter laugh. The Runi could have been lying and a good man, a great man, a man rare in the history of the Magellanics, had been destroyed because he had placed his trust in the alien. It was a bitter and final irony. There remained, however, a shadow of doubt. The Runi might not have acted perversely but because it was his nature to be a gamester, a liar.

Just as it was the nature of Captain Shangrin to be loyal beyond all expectation. Other people's checkmates. Gregory turned to the captain, who appeared to be sleeping, sprawled in his chair, his head forward but his eyes open. He decided to say nothing to him. There was a world where games had rules and players abided by them—Shangrin's world. And there was the real world where rules did not exist. The Runi and Gregory and Smirno and all the others lived in this one. Shangrin was considered crazy because he did not know this, and he would continue not to know. The most important thing in the world for Gregory now was that Shangrin should continue to remain in ignorance.

Very gently he raised the captain's head. His beard was limp and the lines in his face were so deep that the captain might already have aged those two hundred and thirty million years he had so desperately tried to win back by gambling. But his eyes remained clear and childlike. There was not the slightest trace of hardness in them, nor had there ever been. They were a mirror of Shangrin's soul.

He moved his lips and a deep gurgle came up from his lungs. All his muscles seemed flabby, worn out. Finally words formed on his lips, so low that Gregory had to put his ear to the old man's mouth.

"I cheated," Shangrin whispered. "I cheated to beat him and he didn't notice."

The eyes were clear but, as Gregory looked, horrified, they slowly turned up and stared obliquely at the ceiling. Varun Shangrin died. Gregory wept.

They were going home, over the abyss of time.

They were leaving him behind, sole master of his ship, prepared to navigate through time, even though time no longer mattered to him. They were leaving him behind, and it was fitting in a way. It did not imply oblivion, disgrace, condemnation or revenge, or any of those human passions which, in the end, he had mastered. They were leaving him behind because they had to travel another road and in their course through time they could not take the dead with them, nor a ship. They were leaving him behind in the largest, most complex, costliest sarcophagus in the history of the Magellanics. In the misty memories about the legendary planet on which man had first appeared, there were stories of kings who were buried under huge pyramids, and of emperors of the sea whose mortal remains were carried by ships with crimson sails into northern mists, in the land of ice. Shangrin took his place in a long line. . . .

They left him, uncontested master of the past, because the future was opening before them just as the envoys of the future had promised. They had come

back, two of them this time, so alike they might have
been twins. They had wordlessly accepted Gregory's
version of events. They had accepted, without batting
an eye, the Runi's escape. They were certainly skilled
players, good at hiding their reactions.

They had recognized the good faith of the men of
the Magellanics and had offered them, this time with no
strings attached, return to their distant future. Perhaps
they were afraid, Smirno thought as he witnessed their
satisfaction when Gregory accepted, that the turbulent
envoys from the Magellanics would again upset their
plans. They said what had to be said and did what had
to be done. They arranged a rendezvous for the *Vasco*
on the planet they had chosen to shelter, in great crypts,
the field of stasis. For two hundred and thirty million
years, the almost eight thousand passengers of the *Vasco*
would sleep, in a perpetual present, outside the movement of molecules and the intimate dance of matter.

For three days, a continuous stream of men flowed
from the *Vasco*. Gliders filled with passengers in time
filed out, one after another, toward the giant crypts dug
out of the mountains of a small planet in an almost
starless region of space. During the long nights, the
sky remained almost black, and with the day the light
from the distant sun barely pierced the icy clouds which
floated in the high atmosphere.

Smirno was the last to leave the ship. He watched
Gregory and Norma go off on the rocky ledge toward
the last glider. The first mate of the *Vasco* and the
young woman were walking side by side, silently. For a
long time the memory of Shangrin would remain between them, the shadow of madness and greatness.
Then perhaps time and happiness would heal the rift.
It wasn't sure, Smirno said to himself. There were the
makings of a Shangrin in Gregory. Sooner or later he
would set forth again, defying space and time and, if
need be, the law itself, in response to an inner necessity.

What was that necessity, Smirno wondered, which

plucked men from their worlds, their womenfolk, and threw them into the abysses of time and space? Did the masters of time know? Perhaps what they termed the end of history corresponded to the disappearance of that necessity. What can happen to a man in a world in which all planets are known, all destinies understood?

Shangrin had sought the answer, with the Runi, in the game of chess. In one sense, Smirno told himself, Shangrin had found it. As he watched, the enormous, deserted ship rose in the atmosphere like a gigantic bubble, its shadow on the ground growing smaller and finally disappearing in the gray expanse of the sky.

Shangrin had found it whereas he, Smirno, was still seeking it. As he looked into the sky long after the *Vasco* had disappeared, he thought of the identical ship, promised by the envoys of the future, which would take them home.

He had hoped to find peace once the doors of the future had been opened to him. He could again cherish the thought of becoming a xenologist for the central worlds, one of the men who formulated theories and plumbed the mysteries of life and intelligence. He had been successful, after all. He had even had his revenge on Shangrin, for he had been right. But peace eluded him.

The bitterness lingered and, with it, anxiety. He knew now that he had been jealous of Shangrin, of his strength, daring and vitality. He had won, but he had paid dearly for his victory.

He boarded the glider and looked at the arid plain speeding by below them. A few tufts of lichen clung precariously in the interstices of the rocks. He saw the mountains rise in front of them as though they were growing out of the soil then, silently, the great doors of the crypt closed. Now they were going forward in the immense cavern whose walls had been honeycombed into thousands of cells. A Magellanite slept in each of the niches, bathed in cold bluish light. If ever some more complex form of life, groping its way toward intelligence, were to appear in the lichen, this place would appear to it like an underworld, an Elysian field where the gods waited, as they slept, for a rebirth of the world.

He went to his niche. Looking over his shoulder he saw Gregory and Norma kiss and separate. One must go through time alone, he reflected, and yet he knew that billions of creatures would haunt his dreams. One could not glimpse the veiled face of the future with impunity. All the men who would be born one day were now his neighbors—all the men destined to live until the universe was full of them. And not only men, but all peoples . . . the Runis as well as others, the players and the pawns. Perhaps this was what Shangrin had glimpsed.

That completed the picture marvelously, Smirno said to himself bitterly. Just as the sum total of history told a tale, so humans and Runis complemented each other. Without Runis, humans would probably not have achieved one-tenth of their potential. The Runis had momentarily been the ultimate challenge to human civilization, or civilizations, forcing men to outdo themselves.

And war itself, as he now understood it in its multiple variety, need not be murderous. There were infinite ways of waging war, economic, cultural, social, other forms he could not even imagine, with only one point in common, hatred. And he, Smirno, was incapable of judging humans or Runis because it was his nature to be an outsider, an observer, an outcast; in short, a xenologist.

He was sure of only one thing: that for hundreds of years to come, no one would openly question the purpose of the Runis. For a human to do so would be considered worse than murder.

This was the crime which, up to a certain point, he had taxed Shangrin with. He had won out over Shangrin, but it had been an empty victory. He himself was only a bit of flotsam to be washed about by the waves of time for two hundred and thirty million years.

Such were his thoughts as the stasis gripped him and

froze his nerves, for a fraction of eternity, in the blue light. Shangrin had led them to the edge of the regained future, but because he had questioned the gods—and glimpsed something greater and more important than man and Runis together—he had not been allowed to cross the threshold of time. Had he been their victim, their pawn, or had he deliberately chosen his fate? He may have thought he was giving the Runis a handicap by playing his own game, according to his own rules. And he had acted accordingly. He had freed himself, alone, from their hold.

In that respect, at least, Shangrin had won.

Time passed. An invisible finger moved a pawn on the chessboard. Gregory stirred. His lips opened and he murmured: "What time is it?"

In a boundless universe, humanity had appeared.

DAW BOOKS sf

☐ **HUNTERS OF GOR by John Norman.** The eighth novel of the fabulous saga of Tarl Cabot on Earth's orbital twin.
(#UW1102—$1.50)

☐ **HADON OF ANCIENT OPAR by Philip José Farmer.** An epic action-adventure in Atlantean Africa—in the great Burroughs tradition. Fully illustrated.
(#UY1107—$1.25)

☐ **A QUEST FOR SIMBILIS by Michael Shea.** Through the weird world of the Dying Earth they sought for justice.
(#UQ1092—95¢)

☐ **THE BURROWERS BENEATH by Brian Lumley.** A Lovecraftian novel of the men who dared disturb the Earth's subterranean masters.
(#UQ1096—95¢)

☐ **MINDSHIP by Gerald Conway.** The different way of space flight required a mental cork for a cosmic bottle.
(#UQ1095—95¢)

☐ **MIDSUMMER CENTURY by James Blish.** Thrust into the twilight of mankind, he shared a body with an enemy.
(#UQ1094—95¢)

☐ **HOW ARE THE MIGHTY FALLEN by Thomas Burnett Swann.** A fantasy novel of the prehumans and the rise of an exalted legend.
(#UQ1100—95¢)

DAW BOOKS are represented by the publishers of Signet and Mentor Books, THE NEW AMERICAN LIBRARY, INC.

☐ **TRANSIT TO SCORPIO** by Alan Burt Akers. The thrilling saga of Prescot of Antares among the wizards and nomads of Kregen. (#UQ1033—95¢)

☐ **THE SUNS OF SCORPIO** by Alan Burt Akers. Among the colossus-builders and sea raiders of Kregen—the saga of Prescot of Antares II. (#UQ1049—95¢)

☐ **WARRIOR OF SCORPIO** by Alan Burt Akers. Across the Hostile Territories of Kregen—Prescot of Antares III. (#UQ1065—95¢)

☐ **SWORDSHIPS OF SCORPIO** by Alan Burt Akers. A pirate fleet stands between Prescot and the land of his beloved. Prescot of Antares IV. (#UQ1085—95¢)

☐ **PRINCE OF SCORPIO** by Alan Burt Akers. Prescot's greatest battle confronts him in Vallia itself! Prescot of Antares V. (#UY1104—$1.25)

☐ **MANHOUNDS OF ANTARES** by Alan Burt Akers. Dray Prescot on the unknown continent of Havilfar begins a new cycle of Kregen adventures. Scorpio VI. (#UY1124—$1.25)

☐ **ARENA OF ANTARES** by Alan Burt Akers. Dray Prescot confronts strange beasts and fierce men on Havilfar. Scorpio VII. (#UY1145—$1.25)

DAW BOOKS are represented by the publishers of Signet and Mentor Books, THE NEW AMERICAN LIBRARY, INC.

Presenting the international science fiction spectrum:

☐ **THE OVERLORDS OF WAR by Gerard Klein.** Translated by John Brunner, this is a masterpiece of advanced cosmic conception. (#UQ1099—95¢)

☐ **THE DAY BEFORE TOMORROW by Gerard Klein.** To dominate the future, change the past. A prize novel by the "Ray Bradbury" of France. (#UQ1011—95¢)

☐ **STARMASTERS' GAMBIT by Gerard Klein.** Games players of the cosmos—an interstellar adventure equal to the best. (#UQ1068—95¢)

☐ **THE ORCHID CAGE by Herbert W. Franke.** The problem of robots and intelligence as confronted by Germany's master of hard-core science fiction. (#UQ1082—95¢)

☐ **GAMES PSYBORGS PLAY by Pierre Barbet.** They made a whole world their arena and a whole race their pawns. (#UQ1087—95¢)

☐ **HARD TO BE A GOD by A. & B. Strugatski.** A brilliant novel of advanced men on a backward planet—by Russia's most outstanding sf writers. (#UY1141—$1.25)

☐ **THE MIND NET by Herbert W. Franke.** Their starship was kidnapped by an alien brain from a long-dead world. (#UQ1136—95¢)

DAW BOOKS are represented by the publishers of Signet and Mentor Books, THE NEW AMERICAN LIBRARY, INC.
